DE
R

A gripp murder mystery

CHRISTINE GREEN

Kate Kinsella Mysteries Book 10

JOFFE
Ostara
CLASSICS

Revised edition 2024
Joffe Books, London
www.joffebooks.com

First published by Severn House Publishers Ltd
in Great Britain in 2006

This paperback edition was first published
in Great Britain in 2024

Cover art by Cover art by Dee Dee Book Covers

ISBN: 978-1-83526-385-3

CHAPTER ONE

As I walked in the drizzle towards the doctor's surgery, I kept my head down and avoided stepping on the cracks in wet pavements. I hoped it would stop me thinking but it didn't. The sky was as grey as my thoughts and at this moment I felt that the whole world was grey and that I was a lead pencil worn down to the stub with no sharpener in sight.

Hubert, my landlord, is a mixture of friend, colleague and surrogate family and with his part-time help I manage, or did manage, a detective agency. But since my last tragic case I'd merely stuffed myself with comfort food, slept and watched television. Nothing seemed to motivate me and the only reason I was on my way to see the doctor was that Hubert had nagged me consistently for a week and threatened to ask for a home visit. GPs don't do home visits, I told him.

'In that case,' he said, 'you'll get a locum. He might certify you.'

'Don't talk rubbish,' I'd said indignantly but a trickle of doubt had crept in and to pacify Hubert I'd agreed to make an appointment. As an ex-nurse I just knew I'd have a prescription in my hand for the poor man's Prozac within five minutes. I felt that I was zombie-like enough without being medicated but I also knew that anti-depressants do work.

I hadn't seen a GP professionally for some time but the turnover of GPs seemed high, especially at the Health Centre, so I'd opted to change to a more traditional front-room type of surgery. It was situated on the edge of Longborough, a town with no claim to fame and at times so dull a Saturday night's TV seems exciting in contrast. The receptionist was smiley enough but in my low state it made no impression and I sat down to wait my turn with the other glum-looking patients. To add to the general air of gloom, chamber music emanated from a speaker on the wall. There were five of us sat around a table of magazines — six including a snivelling toddler. No one spoke. There was an elderly lady with a walking stick and a heavily bandaged leg, a young girl who nibbled at her nails constantly and a middle-aged man who kept glancing at his wristwatch. The toddler's mother whispered to her child as if a normal voice might shatter the sanctity of the waiting room. As the minutes ticked by I felt more and more depressed. I waited for someone to speak, even just to mention the weather. But no one did. Were they depressed too? Or was the chamber music responsible? I didn't care either way; I just wanted my consultation to be over and done with.

Finally my turn came and I walked in to see a Dr Khan. He was young, handsome, slim and had a smile as bright as sunshine. I guessed he was into his thirties but he seemed to be wearing rather better than me. He had a mature, soothing voice and the moment he asked, 'What's the problem, Kate?' I burst into tears.

When I finally composed myself and was merely sniffing and wiping my eyes he began asking me questions.

'Do you sleep well?'

'All the time.'

'Do you eat well?'

'Ditto.'

He sighed. He began to look older by the minute. 'Have you ever had any thoughts of harming yourself?'

'No! I'm not that depressed.'

'Good,' he murmured. 'So you feel mildly depressed?'

I shrugged. 'I suppose I feel the world is a dark, wicked place and all around me is greyness and misery.'

'What do you think has made you feel like that?'

'My boyfriend was murdered,' I answered bluntly.

'Were you in love with him?'

I shook my head. 'I was very fond of him . . . He wanted to marry me but now . . .' I broke off, unable to get my thoughts together.

'Do you think this loss might be the cause of your depression — that you're actually grieving for him?'

I stared at Dr Khan. Was this grief I was feeling?

'In my opinion,' he said, not waiting for my answer, 'you need to work through your grief. I'm not going to put you on anti-depressants at the moment. I suggest you get some counselling and if possible take a holiday. Please come and see me again if you don't start to feel better soon.'

I felt a real sense of having been cheated as I left the surgery. I clutched no comforting prescription; there would be no long list of side effects to worry about. As I walked along the road the wind whipped up in typical March fashion and I felt angry. My taxes had helped pay for his medical training and he tells me to take a holiday. A holiday alone would surely tip me over my lonely edge. Hubert, being a funeral director, amassed bodies and absorbed other people's grief like particles in a black galactic hole but he *was* needed. He couldn't spare the time to accompany me on holiday. And anyway, if Hubert hadn't recognized that I was grieving then I disputed the young GP's diagnosis.

On the walk back to Humberstone's Funeral Directors my anger began to fade and I got teary again. I felt like a fraud, like I should pull myself together — as if the cure was as simple as stitching together a hand-knit doll. I was falling apart but I wasn't fading away. I wanted to eat and sleep and . . . hibernate. A holiday would only see me eating and drinking even more and would do nothing but accentuate my loneliness.

Hubert was at the door to greet me. 'What did he say?' he asked as Jasper rushed to greet me. Jasper is our shared terrier and I picked him up and snuggled my face into his fur.

'I'll go upstairs,' I muttered, 'and put the kettle on.'

I glanced at Hubert's face; it was full of disappointment. Did he really think I'd be cured by one visit to a doctor?

I made a pot of tea whilst Hubert hovered beside me waiting for me to tell him word for word what the doctor had actually said. I didn't feel like talking but eventually I said, 'Dr Khan thinks I should go on holiday. I suppose being young he thinks a holiday can sort everything.'

'He must have said something else. What about anti-depressants?'

I sat down with my tea and took two chocolate biscuits from the biscuit tin. 'He didn't seem to think I was depressed enough to need them.'

'In that case,' snapped Hubert, 'you conned him. I've seen the change in you.'

I was busy wolfing down the biscuits. I didn't care what Hubert thought.

'You're keeping something back, Kate,' he said, placing an arm around me. 'I know you are. Come on, tell Uncle Hubert.'

'All right . . . I give up,' I said eventually, swallowing hard to avoid more tears. 'The doc thinks I'm grieving and it should be allowed to run its course. But losing David wasn't like losing a husband or life-long partner. It was a terrible shock, but . . .'

'I should have recognized it,' murmured Hubert. 'Bereavement takes many forms. I've known people to grieve for months for their deceased budgerigar.' He added hurriedly, 'I don't mean David was worth less than a budgerigar, but any loss is personal.'

'Yeah, I suppose so,' I said as I rummaged in the biscuit tin for the remaining biscuits.

'Stuffing your face,' said Hubert in a less kindly tone, 'won't help.'

'It can and it does,' I said.

'Did the doc recommend counselling?' he asked.

I nodded.

'You should think about that.'

'I have and I don't want some softly spoken therapist listening to my innermost thoughts.'

'Well, you can't just wallow in misery for ever,' said Hubert, removing the biscuit tin. 'You'll get so fat you'll be wanting liposuction.'

'Leave me alone,' I snapped as I flounced off to my bedroom. Jasper, sensing my mood, didn't follow.

* * *

For three days I left my room only to raid the fridge and cook snacks like cheese on toast and thick porridge with cream and sugar. If I'd had the energy I'd have walked to the baker's for cream cakes but I didn't even have to walk Jasper because Hubert had arranged for the staff to walk him.

On the evening of the third day Hubert came knocking on my door and didn't even wait for my reply. I'd been eating a crisp sandwich in bed wearing a tattered old tee shirt and a grey cardigan of Hubert's that was years past its best and had been destined for the bin.

'Enough is enough is enough,' he said importantly, as if it were a political mantra. 'I've arranged for a holiday for you with plenty of company and hardly any travelling. It's four star, the food is supposed to be excellent and it's paid for . . . so I don't want any arguments. I'll be taking you tomorrow.'

I didn't have time to respond. I sat up, my mouth gritty with crisps, and was about to say, 'No way,' when Hubert simply walked out.

Later that evening, having given some thought to four-star meals and accommodation, I began to think it might be a good idea. I was going slightly stir crazy and a change of scene might just do me good. I had a bath and then raided my drawers for some relatively new nightwear and knickers that weren't so small that they dropped over my belly to resemble a pubic tourniquet. I wasn't, after all, expecting any encounters but there could be a fire drill or even a fire so it was best to be prepared.

In the kitchen I found Hubert deep into a mega Sudoku.

'I can't crack this one,' he said despondently.

'Well, you've cracked it with me,' I said. 'I will go tomorrow, but what is this holiday? It isn't some sort of adventure or learn-to-paint-landscapes holiday, is it?'

'No, it's a hotel that's . . . restful.'

'I do nothing but rest here.'

'There you'll have your meals cooked and you'll meet people.'

'I don't want to meet people but I suppose I could just avoid the other guests and have room service.'

'You could,' he said. 'But either way it'll make a change.'

'And you won't have to see my miserable face for . . . How long am I going for?'

He paused before saying, 'Three weeks.'

'Three weeks! I don't suppose I'll stand it for one week never mind three.'

'You need some time away from here. Let's face it, Kate, this is a house of the dead. I forget that you weren't brought up with it as I was.'

I sighed. I didn't have the energy to argue and maybe Hubert did have a point. A change of scene might just improve my mood.

'OK, I'll go but I'll pay for it myself. I can't let you subsidize me all the time.'

'It's my treat. I can afford it and you can't.'

'How much is it?'

'Expensive. But then I think you're worth it. You can pay me back by coming home cheerful and getting in the clients again.'

I smiled wearily. I really thought my days of stumbling investigations had come to an end. There was only one problem with that. My capabilities, whatever they were, didn't seem to belong in the market place. Texting is something I haven't mastered yet; I can't set a video to record and my computer skills are very basic. I'm neither smart nor dynamic and my organisational skills are probably on a par with a motherless chimp's. Even as I mused I realized that my low self-esteem, although never high, had plummeted since David had died. I felt responsible and he was the second man in my life who had died. The first, Mike, died as a result of a random accident so at least I felt no sense of guilt there, but with David I did.

'We'll be leaving at ten thirty tomorrow so you'll have to rouse yourself,' said Hubert with a brief smile.

CHAPTER TWO

My mild euphoria didn't last, however, and after a hot bath I languished on the bed and had fallen asleep only to be awakened by Hubert cheerfully calling out that it was seven thirty.

Dragging myself into the kitchen like an overweight sloth I was met by Hubert thrusting a mug of tea into my hand and informing me smugly that he'd made sandwiches, filled a flask with coffee and had also made travel contingency plans according to instructions from the TV weather person.

'Weather forecast isn't good,' he said. 'There could even be snow on high ground.'

'It's supposed to be spring,' I grumbled.

'Spring could be late where we're going,' muttered Hubert with his back towards me as he retrieved toast from the toaster.

'My hearing's very acute,' I said. 'You'd better tell me where I'm being taken. I may be depressed but I haven't totally lost the will to live.'

'North Wales.'

I allowed the information to sink in. 'My will to live,' I said slowly, 'is fast ebbing away.'

'Don't moan,' he said as he thrust a plate of well-buttered toast into my hand. 'You can imagine you're somewhere else.'

'When the mist falls in North Wales,' I said, 'on the rocks and the crags and where there's no sign of civilisation for miles, it needs more than my feeble imagination to transport me to somewhere more . . .'

'Sexy?'

'More *cheerful,* I was going to say, but I mustn't be ungrateful even though I don't want to go.'

'Eat your toast,' said Hubert. 'I'll pack the car and we'll be off in half an hour.'

Jasper lay at my feet. I bent down and stroked his head and told him Hubert would be back and that one of the lads would walk him soon. He may not have understood my words but he knew that luggage meant someone was going away and since his bed and bowl were still in place it wasn't going to be him. He gazed up at me sadly and I felt a real pang of guilt for I hadn't given him much attention over the last few weeks, but he had remained constantly by my side as if to reassure me.

* * *

I dozed in the car as Hubert drove and occasionally surfaced to notice that the nearer we got to the Welsh border the murkier the weather became. The fine rain mixed with wintry gloom and a pall of mist on higher ground seemed an omen of more bad weather to come.

The journey once across the border had been punctuated with traffic hold-ups of unknown origin, road works and a lorry that had shed its load. After two hours of driving and an hour at a standstill I was longing to whine, 'Are we nearly there?' but I kept quiet because after all Hubert would have to drive back by himself and his time really was valuable.

'It's only a few more miles,' said Hubert as we passed a signpost for Bala.

'Where are we looking for?'

There was a long pause before he mumbled, 'I'll look at the map.'

We stopped in a lay-by and Hubert stared intently at the map and at internet directions. He was wearing new bifocals and I wasn't sure he could actually see the small print.

'Let me have a look,' I said. 'What's the name of the nearest town?'

'It's isolated. The nearest village is about three miles from . . .' He broke off.

'From where?' I asked, getting slightly irritated at Hubert's reticence which was now bordering on the shifty.

'I've found it,' he said, peering at the map.

'Show me.'

He pointed to a symbol in the middle of nowhere. 'That's it,' he said.

I stared at the symbol. 'You're mad,' I spluttered. 'If you think I'm staying there for three weeks . . .'

'Stop panicking. OK, it's a church, but it is deconsecrated. Now it's a retreat — Peace Haven Retreat.'

'You told me,' I said accusingly, 'that it was a luxury hotel, not some old church offering quiet contemplation.'

'Don't prejudge, Kate. They are very fussy who they take.'

'They can't be that fussy if they're taking me.'

We drove on for a few more isolated miles of narrow lanes with the mist and murk turning to rain that battered the already struggling daffodil stalks growing haphazardly on the roadside. Then through the rain I finally saw a church steeple. I knew most of Wales had chapels rather than churches but as we drew closer I could see this was a large traditional Anglo-Saxon church set amongst pine trees and the remains of old gravestones. I looked in vain for a sign that mentioned four stars or Peace Haven Retreat but there was no such sign. The stained-glass windows were dulled through lack of sunlight and the oak door was recessed in a dark porch.

Hubert parked the car and I could now see there was a more modern brick extension at the side of the church. That didn't lift my spirits and I sat morosely in the car whilst Hubert got out, opened the boot, removed my two pieces of luggage and placed them by the church's front door. I was beginning to wonder if this church was more derelict than deconsecrated. There was no one to be seen and no cars. Hubert signalled to me get out of the car and reluctantly I did, although my instincts were in cut-and-run mode.

At the church door — which looked strong enough to survive a battering ram — a ship's bell and a heavy iron knocker caused Hubert a momentary quandary.

'I'll ring the bell and you knock,' I said.

The response was so prompt it was as if we were expected to arrive at that very moment; either that or we'd been seen. I hardly noticed the man who opened the door because I looked straight past him to what I expected to be an interior like some village hall.

'Hang on a sec,' said the man. 'Switch on, Dave,' he yelled. A second later the lights came on. The village hall suddenly seemed more like the Albert Hall. The vast domed ceilings were lit by a myriad lights reminding me of those mock medieval banqueting rooms. The stained-glass windows were lit by up-lighters and the sheer size of the place caused both of us to fall silent. As we stood there with our mouths slightly open a tall man in his early thirties walked towards us. I was aware then that I took a sharp intake of breath. He was wearing a long purple kaftan and sandals.

'I'm off,' I muttered as I turned back towards the door.

Hubert's hand, as quick as a cobra, grabbed mine. 'You're staying,' he said, grimly determined.

The man gripped me in a firm handshake. 'You must be Kate,' he said, smiling broadly. 'Welcome. I'm Zoton.'

And I'm the bloody Queen of Sheba, I thought, but Hubert was hanging on to me tightly so I managed a weak smile and decided I could leave at any time.

'I'll show you round,' said Zoton. 'Dave our porter-cum-handyman will take your luggage upstairs to your room.' His gaze went upwards to the galleried floors. 'You're in room three on the first floor.'

Hubert let go of my hand. 'I'm going now, Kate. I have to get back.' Zoton shook Hubert's hand and I walked out to the porch with Hubert. I didn't want to stay and as I hugged Hubert goodbye I could feel tears welling in my eyes. 'You'll be fine,' he said, patting my shoulder. 'It's got a good reputation, this place.'

'What for?'

'Don't be difficult. Just try to enjoy yourself.'

Zoton took my elbow and began his guided tour. The ground floor of the former church was a spacious open-plan area that had been sectioned off by various screens.

'This is obviously the lounge,' said Zoton, parting an olive-green screen and indicating deep pile carpets and four three-seater sofas in chocolate brown. We then moved on to the games area, and the sight of a table-tennis table and a dart board didn't thrill me.

'And this is the garden room,' said Zoton proudly, showing me bamboo chairs and sofas amongst a vast array of greenery and palms. I said nothing. I still wanted out and the appearance of a grey-haired woman with severely scraped-back hair, a thin smile and an identical purple kaftan did nothing to reassure me.

'What the hell is this place?' I asked, now becoming really rattled.

'I'm Rogon,' said the woman. 'Peace Haven is a therapy centre for people who have been through particularly traumatic events and need help to rebuild their lives. Our hopes and our aims are to send you away from here with a sense of inner peace and purpose. Healed, hopefully.'

'So you're therapists?'

She nodded. 'There are three resident therapists, all qualified psychologists. One of the reasons we wear our uniform is so that we are immediately recognisable.'

You're certainly that, I thought.

'I expect you're feeling a little disorientated,' said Rogon in a soft I'm-a-kind-and-caring-person tone. 'There's always tea and coffee available in the refectory — that'll make you feel better.'

'I'd prefer a double brandy,' I said only half seriously.

'There is no alcohol allowed on the premises,' she said sternly. 'We do have guests who have problems with alcohol.'

'Tea will be fine then,' I said crisply, already longing for something alcoholic.

Zoton informed me in the refectory that the other guests were expected shortly. I sat alone at the solid oak table that could comfortably sit twelve, feeling awkward and ill at ease.

'We're serving a snack meal at two today,' he said. 'Usually lunch is at one, tea at four thirty and supper at seven thirty.' I glanced at my watch. It was twelve forty-five and I was hungry. Rogon had disappeared and at the beeping sound emanating from somewhere in his kaftan, Zoton excused himself. 'I'll send Dave in and he'll take you up to your room.'

A few minutes later Dave appeared. He was in his sixties, slightly stooped and with straggly hair and eyebrows to match.

'Come on then, sweetheart, follow me,' he said cheerfully.

He seemed to struggle with my luggage but I didn't offer to help, thinking I might damage his self-esteem; after all he was a porter.

My bedroom was small and restful in shades of palest green. It wasn't a nun's cell but it was certainly basic. A bible sat on my bedside table and there was no television or radio. Dave put down the luggage and said, 'When you 'ear the gong it means grub's up. Don't be late because the chef's a miserable bugger — good cook but has a bit of a history, if you know what I mean.' I nodded as if I did, but of course I was none the wiser. I liked Dave though; he seemed normal, he wore normal clothes and had a normal name. As he left he said, 'I'd keep your door locked if I was you, sweetheart. You never know.'

The gong sounded an hour later. I was about to meet more strangers — traumatized strangers — and somehow the gong's resonant tones caused me to shudder. I took a few deep breaths and went down to join my new companions.

CHAPTER THREE

By the time I reached the refectory I was the last to arrive or so I was told by the overweight chef who was piling the table with soup, home-made bread, assorted cold meats and salad.

'You're the last,' he said. 'Enjoy!' In any other circumstances I might have either been counting the calories or thinking *just go for it!* As the other guests sat down I realized I'd lost my appetite. There were three men and two women. We sat down in silence, three on one side of the refectory table and three on the other. I glanced around, looking for a host, but there was no sign of Zoton and Rogon.

'Shall I be mother?' asked a round-faced man with a pony tail and a less than masculine voice. We began passing him our soup bowls to be filled from a tureen placed in the centre of the table. 'I'm Howard, by the way — known as Howard the Coward to my friends.'

'I'm Kate,' I murmured. The man to my right put out his hand. He was young, black and gorgeous. 'I'm Wayne McKenzie . . .' He paused as if I should have recognized his name. 'The actor,' he supplied. The name meant nothing to me and if I'd seen him on television I was sure I would have remembered him. His hand felt warm and strong and in response to his lovely smile I found myself smiling with no effort at all.

On my left sat a busty woman wearing a low-cut blouse and tight jeans and with long blonde hair that flopped over her eyes. She seemed to wink at me with her one exposed eye. 'Funny place this,' she said. 'I'm Cheryl. I'm a model.' Then she added in a whisper, 'Or I was once.'

Across the table a scruffy-looking man in his thirties muttered, 'Hi, I'm Blake.' The woman next to him was thin, verging on dangerously so, and as pale as bloodless gums. 'I'm Fran. I . . .' She broke off to sip her soup.

The silence that followed was broken moments later with the slap of sandals on parquet flooring and Zoton and Rogon appeared on the lower gallery accompanied by a tall man with a shaggy grey beard who was wearing a black kaftan.

'Does he think he's Dracula?' asked Cheryl.

'More like Gandalf,' said Howard.

'Who the hell is Gandalf?' she replied.

The man in black, his purple-clad cohorts by his side, stood at the head of the table, spread his arms wide and said in a gravelly voice, 'Welcome . . . welcome to you all.' There was a pause before he said, 'My name is Argon. I'm the leader of the team and my time is yours. My office is on the top gallery and is always open.' From his voluminous kaftan he produced sheets of paper. 'The facilities and opportunities of Peace Haven are clearly laid out. Each afternoon various treatments and beauty therapies are available. Those rooms are on the ground floor and are kept locked until two p.m. During the morning we have One to One Time.' He paused again. 'This enables two guests at a time to share an activity and is followed by half an hour or so with one of us three with the funny names. When we first started here we used our own names but after a nasty incident we decided to use false names and be clearly recognisable by our clothing.' He stared at each one of us before asking, 'Any questions?'

No one spoke. An air of slight depression seemed to have descended. Finally the scruffy guy, Blake, said, 'So can we opt out of activities if we want to?'

Argon fixed him with his beady grey eyes. 'You have all been selected because of past traumas and tragedies. Some of you are self-funding. You owe it to yourselves and others to make the most of this time. You can be assured we will help you with your future life choices but we all need to work together.' He paused again as if to gauge our reaction, which was zilch. 'Tomorrow at nine,' he continued, 'I'll be giving you a short motivational talk after breakfast and we'll be handing out journals that we hope you'll keep during your time here. For the moment please just get to know each other.'

I sighed inwardly but we dutifully started reading our daily routine for the next three weeks as the gruesome threesome padded away. They seemed a humourless trio and I didn't look forward to either tomorrow or the next day. Our spirits plummeted further when we learned that there was no signal in the area for using our mobile phones.

'What time's tea?' asked Cheryl.

'It says here four thirty,' said Wayne. 'I suppose it's when we hear the gong.'

'See you later,' I said as I made for my room.

I sat on my bed and read the information about Peace Haven carefully. Sure enough there in the small print were several little gems I'd missed at first reading. Apart from the lack of mobile phone signal there were no newspapers available or television or radio. After a while the quietness made me restless so I paced the room for a while and then stared out of my small oval window. It was still light but grey and cloudy and the few daffodils on the lawn area drooped dismally.

I lay down on the bed, staring at the ceiling, and thought about the other guests, putting them into categories. There was the cheerful gay hairdresser, the slightly dim model, the less-than-well-known actor, the depressed career woman with anorexia, Blake the mystery scruff and me the fat depressive. What did we all add up to? Becoming more and more suspicious, I was furious with Hubert. He must have known and I was desperate now to speak to him and yell at him for misleading me. My fury quickly dwindled to anxiety and I told myself that I was getting paranoid. There must be an explanation and somewhere a land line, I reasoned, so I left my room and made my way downstairs to find out where.

In the dining area the table had been laid for the evening meal and from the kitchen I could hear clattering sounds. I knocked on the door but there was no response so I opened the door to be greeted by a shout of, 'Clear off — no guests are allowed in the kitchen.'

I swore and walked away to look for the handyman, Dave, who seemed the only friendly person in the place. I eventually found him in a cubby hole near the front door. He sat at small table reading the *Sun* newspaper and his embarrassment was as severe as if I'd found him naked having sex with a nubile young woman. Hurriedly he shoved the newspaper under the table. 'What can I do for you, sweetheart?' he said.

'I wanted to use a phone to ring my . . . boss to make sure he arrived home in one piece.'

Dave scratched his ear. 'You catch Argon later on and be nice to him and he might let you use the phone in his office.'

'Why the problem with using a phone?' I asked.

'No idea, sweetheart, but sometimes the guests get unsettled and it can cause problems.'

'This is a really strange place,' I said. 'How long have you worked here?'

'Only a month, love. See here, we work three weeks on — that's the length of stay — and then we have a week off, so I'm still finding my feet, so to speak.'

'Do you live locally?'

He shook his head. 'Can't you tell I'm not Welsh? I'm a Londoner. I've got a room not much bigger than a box in the extension.'

'And that's where you live?'

'Yeah. Suits me fine. I'm getting on in years. The work isn't heavy and the food's good so I'm sorted.' I was about to ask how on earth a sixty-year-old Londoner had landed up in such a strange place but a buzzer sounded and a red light shone just above the door and he muttered, 'Gotta go, love, that's the boss wanting me.' He ushered me from his office and locked the door behind him. When he was out of sight I tried the front door; it was bolted with original-looking bolts at the top and bottom.

I began walking back to my room but I felt anxious, as if I were a young child left in a boarding school with no real understanding of why, not knowing when, if ever, I'd see my parents again.

Back in my room I told myself not to be such a wimp. There were six guests and I told myself we could always mutiny. The front door couldn't be the only door as it would never pass the fire regulations, unless of course deconsecrated churches were exempt. The kitchen must have a door and somewhere there was an exit point to the new extension. There was no need to panic and although I still wanted to speak to Hubert, at least I now didn't want to deafen him with a tirade.

I decided to forgo tea, ignoring the gong, and by the time seven thirty came I was actually waiting for the gong as I was feeling a bit peckish. It sounded just after seven forty.

The trio were in position by the table welcoming us by shaking hands and directing us to our places so that we sat next to someone different. This time Blake was on my right and Fran was to my left. We all tried to smile and then quite abruptly I said, so that the others could hear, 'Argon, I want to make a phone call after supper — where can I do that?' His answering expression said *troublemaker* but he forced a smile and said, 'Would anyone else like to use the phone?' To my amazement no one did. Not a soul responded. 'I'll leave my office door open, Kate — top floor, room one.' Not so difficult then, but asking permission each time was going to be a pain. There had to be a way. Somewhere locally there was bound to be a phone box or a pub with a phone. Tomorrow I'd investigate. I smiled to myself; from investigating murder I was reduced to trying to find a phone.

I'd had a feeling that the dubious three might eat with us but they left with a cheery *bon appétit* and the chef appeared to serve us with another tureen of soup from which we helped ourselves.

'What is it?' asked Fran as she poked her thick soup suspiciously with her spoon.

The soup was faintly orange. 'My guess is pumpkin,' I said, 'but to be honest it doesn't taste of much.'

Fran ate her soup in slow motion, sip by painful sip. 'I don't have much of an appetite,' she explained although it was perfectly obvious. Blake on my right had finished his soup and was already on his second bread roll.

'I could do with a glass of wine,' said Howard. 'I don't drink much but in a situation like this . . .' He tailed off but we knew exactly what he meant.

It was Cheryl who spoke next. In a whisper she said, 'I've got some vodka with me.'

'Ooh, you little devil,' said Norman. 'Where is it?'

'In my room. Shall I get it? I could put it in an Evian bottle.'

'Why not?' said Blake. 'Go for it, girl.'

Cheryl left the table and returned a few minutes later empty-handed and looking anxious.

'It's gone — I've looked everywhere. There were two bottles. They're both gone.'

'Bloody cheek!' said Howard.

Fran put down her spoon. 'We were told there was to be no alcohol. It could cause trouble.'

There was a collective sigh but Cheryl looked near to tears and Howard gave her a little pat on the back and murmured, 'We'll sue the buggers when we get out of here.'

The main course was either salmon or risotto. The chef may have been unfriendly and temperamental but he was a great cook and our mood had slightly lifted by the time a choice of two desserts arrived. Fran toyed with all three courses and Blake ate everything at speed. Conversation revolved around the food and it was obvious that everyone including me wanted to stay in their protective shell.

Just before the coffee arrived I excused myself and made my way to the top floor of the gallery. The door to Argon's office was slightly ajar. I walked inside, closed the door and looked round. There was a traditional desk with a phone, two chairs and a pot plant. There was no computer, filing cabinet or papers.

I sat at the desk and lifted the receiver. Something small caught my eye just above the door. It was round and had a slight glint in the middle — just like an eye. I was right.

I dialled Hubert's number. Maybe he was totally innocent, I told myself.

He seemed pleased to hear from me. Jasper was fine, the journey back had been easy.

'How did you find this place?' I asked.

'I told you — on the internet.'

'That's not a recommendation, Hubert. You can learn how to make bombs on the internet.'

'What's happened? What's the matter?'

'Staying here are a gay hairdresser, a failing actor, a glamour model, a mystery scruff, a nervous career woman with anorexia and me, the fat depressive. What does that sound like to you?'

'A cross section.' Then he added, 'And you're not fat.'

'That's not the point I'm making. If you add a CCTV camera, maybe several, and three so-called counsellors with funny names who wear kaftans, what does that sound like to you?

'What am I supposed to say, Kate? I know the organisation seemed fussy about who they accepted.'

'I'm not being paranoid,' I said defensively, 'but I think we're being filmed and this is the latest reality TV show, like *Big Brother*.'

'You're losing it,' said Hubert. 'Anyway you're not a celebrity.'

'Since when has that mattered? It's being a failure as a celebrity that matters. If you're successful why go on such a programme?'

'They can't show you on TV without your permission, so stop worrying. And reality TV doesn't charge luxury hotel rates to take part. The participants get paid.'

I fell silent. Eventually I said, 'I think in that case we're part of some weird experiment and someone is going to get tipped over the edge.'

'Just make sure it isn't you,' said Hubert, sounding worried.

At the moment there was a clattering sound from downstairs. I left the phone and went out to the gallery and looked down. Someone was on the floor and the chef was yelling to everyone to stand back.

'I must go,' I said hurriedly to Hubert and put down the phone.

On my way downstairs I worked out, by a process of elimination, that it was Cheryl lying on the floor.

CHAPTER FOUR

By the time I got to the ground floor the kaftan gang had also arrived. Cheryl lay on the floor but was stirring and looking around her. 'What happened?' she asked, her eyes unfocused.

Howard knelt beside her and said, 'Dunno. One minute you were on the chair, the next you were on the floor.'

Argon stepped forward. 'You need to be in your bed now. Who would you like to take you there?'

'Kate,' she said, struggling to get up. We helped her up but as we did so her pallor increased and she was trembling. I took one arm and Howard took the other. As we slowly moved away I heard Argon encouraging everyone else to 'enjoy themselves'.

At Cheryl's bedroom door Howard left us. I sat Cheryl on the bed and closed the door.

'I feel a bloody fool,' she said. 'I could do with a drink.'

'We all could.'

'No,' she said. 'I drink every day. This is the longest I've gone without a drink in months.' She collapsed back against the pillows, which was probably a mistake because the next second she was beginning to puke into her hands. I ran to get a bath towel and managed to catch most of it. Cheryl was shaking now and beads of sweat appeared on her forehead.

'Have I got the bed in a mess?' she asked. I reassured her and put a chair in the bathroom, sluiced the towel in the lavatory bowl and then escorted her to the chair.

'I'll help you get undressed,' I said. Cheryl raised her arms so that I could take off her turquoise sweater that looked like cashmere and was now speckled with vomit. I undid her bra and as I did so she crossed her arms but not before I'd seen the scars. I was used to hiding my feelings about wounds and sores and deformity, so I said quietly, 'Was that botched surgery?'

She lowered her hands and turned towards me. 'No, darling, that was my ex-husband.' Now I could see clearly that her breasts were covered in stab wounds. She undid her jeans and showed me more on her abdomen. 'I only survived thanks to the NHS.'

'You don't have to talk about it,' I said.

'No, I want to. It's one of the reasons I'm here.'

'To convalesce?'

'No, to hide. He's being released from prison tomorrow. He got seven years, he's served four.'

'But you're only here for three weeks — what then?'

'I thought this place might get me off the booze and give me confidence.'

'Why did you bring the vodka then?'

'I'm weak or I wouldn't have stayed with that mad bastard, would I? I thought bringing it would be some sort of test — bloody daft idea.'

'Not really,' I said. 'Only like an ex-smoker hiding their last packet of fags and then one day succumbing.'

Cheryl's colour had improved. She washed her face, cleaned her teeth, slipped on a silk nightie and looked normal again. Unusually she looked younger and prettier without make-up. 'I'm twenty-eight,' she said. 'I feel fifty. My glamour modelling days are over. I'm living on my credit cards and I know he'll come after me.'

'He has to find you first.'

'Yeah,' she said. 'But he's mad and bloody clever.'

'You need to get some sleep. This place is very secure and in a few days you could feel much stronger.'

'I hope you're right. I'm an Essex girl and we're meant to be feisty but I feel like a kitten being chased by a Rottweiler — he even looks like a Rottweiler, the ugly bastard!'

It didn't seem the right time to ask why she'd married him in the first place so I said goodnight and told her I'd see her in the morning.

'If I'm climbing the walls can I come to your room?'

'Of course,' I said, not sure it was such a good idea. 'Lock your door when I leave. You'll feel safe then.'

She didn't look convinced; she looked scared and very alone.

Back in my room I locked my door and planned a little sabotage. I rummaged in my handbag and found a piece of chewing gum. I chewed it for a few moments then took a chair and stood on it by the door. By stretching my arm my hand could reach the darkest recess of the coving just above the door. It was the smallest CCTV camera I'd ever seen but it wouldn't be spying on me tonight. I slipped the chewing gum from my mouth and stuck it on the camera lens. The fit was perfect. My privacy was restored and I felt a little sense of triumph because I was beating the system, whatever that system was.

The night was silent and I slept well and woke feeling moderately cheerful.

Just after an almost-silent breakfast Zoton handed us each a health questionnaire to be filled in later and told us who was to be our 'One to One' partner. Argon's motivational talk would start at ten thirty. I was partnered with Howard, Fran was with Blake. Cheryl, who looked much perkier this morning, was twinned with the handsome Wayne. She winked at me as she walked off with him.

Howard and I were directed by Rogon to a room on the ground floor. Apart from two swivel chairs, a table and a lamp the room was empty. Except, that is, for a large box wrapped in gold paper that was sitting on the table.

'You play pass the parcel,' said Rogon. 'Unwrap each layer carefully. You'll find a question in each one and you are to answer and discuss each one. We would like this to take about an hour and then we'll arrange an individual counselling session.' Rogon forced a smile.

'You're a bundle of laughs, love,' said Howard. 'Do we get any music for passing the parcel?'

'No. Please take this seriously.' She was obviously peeved and seemed a little nervous and I had the feeling she was very new to the job. Her disappointed facial expression reminded me of a young teacher on teaching practice faced with little devils when she expected little angels.

Howard's roundish face broke into a wide grin but then he looked serious. 'We'll do this task,' he said slowly. 'As a matter of life and death.'

Rogon cast him a withering glance as she and her kaftan flounced out.

'Ladies first,' said Howard.

The parcel was fixed with sellotape and, as carefully as I could, I removed the first layer.

'We could do with a drum roll at the very least,' said Howard. There was a slip of paper inside and I paused slightly before opening it. 'Did you know there are cameras everywhere?' I asked.

He nodded. 'I wouldn't be surprised if we weren't wired for sound too. So be careful what you say.'

'Why would they do that?'

He shrugged. 'No idea. Read the question, my lovely.'

I read out the question: 'What is your idea of the perfect holiday?' It seemed innocuous enough.

'Well, it's not this one, is it?' said Howard. 'My idea of a perfect holiday includes buckets of alcohol, good food, sunshine and more to the point a bit of congenial company.'

'I'd agree with that. I get bored with beach holidays and I've always fancied pony trekking in Andalusia.'

Howard removed the next piece of wrapping paper and read out the question: 'Have you ever been in love? They've got a bloody cheek. I've had enough of this. Let's just open the box and ignore the questions.'

Howard was obviously rattled and he began tearing at the paper and casting aside the questions until he got to the last layer and the final small box. Inside were two gold-wrapped chocolates. We ate our chocolates and then burst out laughing. The tension was gone now and we glanced at our watches and talked politics for a while and then I asked Howard about hairdressing.

'It's great. I love it. Every day is different but then I'm more of a barber — it's male hairdressing I do which includes facials and manicures these days . . . And what about you, Kate? What do you do?'

'I run an investigation agency with the help of my landlord, Hubert, but I'm not sure if I'm going to continue with it.'

'Why's that?'

'I'm not very good and my last case wrecked my confidence.' I didn't want to say any more than that but perhaps if Howard had opened up a little I might have said more. Whatever had driven him here must have affected him badly. His reaction to the question about being in love made me suspect that perhaps his partner had died.

'Yeah,' he said. 'I know what you mean.'

I wondered how he could know — after all hairdressing, although hard on the feet and back, wasn't exactly dangerous. I didn't press him to explain; our hour was up and we had to vacate the room.

We all met up in the lounge area and there was a buzz, albeit a disgruntled one, and Blake was complaining that he'd wanted to go for a walk and the front door was locked and bolted.

'They're treating us like bloody prisoners. We're paying them, after all. We could be staying at the Ritz for this sort of money.'

Everyone nodded in agreement but then Argon swept towards us. 'Sit down, everyone.' We sat on the sofas and waited expectantly. 'We know some guests,' he said, 'are unhappy about our security arrangements. The front door will now be unlocked on request but otherwise will remain locked. Some people here need to feel secure and to this end Peace Haven has CCTV in every room. This is not so that we can spy on you but so that you can feel safe.'

I looked round my fellow guests. I could understand Cheryl wanting to feel safe, but the others? What the hell or who the hell were they scared of? And was I the odd one out? Was I here for a reason? Don't be silly, I told myself, why would anyone want a depressed, burnt-out private investigator? Even if I was some sort of plant, what was I supposed to investigate?

CHAPTER FIVE

The suspicious mutterings of my mind continued for a while but eventually I came back to the real world to try to concentrate on Argon's supposed motivational talk. He used words like *proactive*, *denial*, *confrontational*, *victimise*, but trying to suck up chocolate through a straw would have motivated me more.

He did warn us not to divulge any personal information to the external staff. 'Just like in the Second World War, careless talk costs lives.' He paused for that to sink in. 'Now then, what are you going to choose: the positive or the negative?' He paused again. 'What do you choose?' No one spoke. He repeated the question. Still no response. 'Come on,' he said. 'Speak up!'

On the third request we obediently said, 'The positive.'

He seemed satisfied. I wasn't. I thought a Longborough plumber could have put together a better talk. It made me doubt he was qualified in either counselling or psychology. If I could have used my mobile I'd have contacted Hubert there and then to check him out. But since he didn't have a proper name neither option was possible.

My thoughts were interrupted by our rotund chef shouting, 'Coffee's up.'

We grouped ourselves around the coffee jugs in the dining area. 'I thought that was quite good,' said Cheryl.

'How's it going to help you?' asked Wayne.

She shrugged. 'I dunno. You've got to try to be strong, haven't you?'

Wayne looked upwards towards the stained-glass window. Outside it was grey and I knew instinctively that his thoughts were grey too.

Spirits lifted a little over our coffee and biscuits as our three so-called counsellors drifted away. So far they were as convincing as elderly deaf nuns auditioning for a West End musical.

'You look down in the mouth, Kate,' said Howard, holding out the plate of biscuits.

'I was just wondering about our counsellors' credentials. I didn't book this . . . event myself, you see, and it's wall to wall weird, isn't it?'

Howard put down the biscuits and took my hands in his. 'Go with the flow, dear heart,' he said softly. 'Go with the flow.'

He joined Fran then and I looked around for someone to talk to. Only Blake stood alone, his back pressed against a wall. When I approached he looked nervous; beads of sweat had appeared on his forehead. 'Are you feeling OK?' I asked.

'I just want out of here. I'm beginning to feel claustrophobic.'

'We could go for a walk.'

'We've got counselling sessions now.'

'We could bunk off,' I suggested.

He thought about that for a few moments. Although he didn't look the type to stick to the rules, he was making it obvious he really didn't want to rock the organisation.

'If I get the key,' I said, 'you could follow me out.'

'You're right,' he said after a long pause. 'First day and I'm finding it hard to cope. I've got to get out for a breath of air.' Then he added, 'Sod it anyway. I don't need to talk to these bloody do-gooders.'

About five minutes later I came across Zoton who was accompanying Fran for her first counselling session. Her eyes were downcast and her footsteps slow as if she were reluctantly being taken away for interrogation. I smiled, hoping to look reassuring. She managed a fleeting smile in return. I noticed her brown eyes looked dead, as if all hope had left them.

I asked Zoton about the key, which to my surprise he already had in his hand. 'It's raining,' he said. 'You'll need an umbrella.' As they walked away I had an uneasy feeling and yet I couldn't think why. After all there was sure to be more than one key and he'd given it freely.

Outside the weather came as a shock. Inside the church the weather held no importance and the rain couldn't be heard, but outside it was tipping down. Blake either didn't have an umbrella or wanted to appear macho. He wore a black padded jacket and as we walked the path through grass mounds and the occasional old gravestone his shoulders straightened and he took several deep breaths. Then as we left the church yard he stopped, turned his face to the sky and let the rain pour down his face. I stood by his side hearing the rain hit my brolly whilst Blake's face reflected pure bliss. 'I love rain,' he said.

We walked on in silence, the only view being sweeping green hillsides and trees. After walking some distance and finding the air more cold than fresh I said, 'It seems a bit pointless to go on. There's no sign of civilization.'

'What did you expect? Starbucks and a Marks and Spencer?'

'No. A pub at the very least.'

'They wouldn't be open anyway.'

The silence and the tramping through puddles continued. The wind seemed to be whipping up and Peace Haven and lunch seemed a far better option at that moment. My legs were getting tired and my thoughts now were on the walk back rather than the walk forward. A bit like getting old, I guessed. I looked at my watch. We'd been out for an hour and Blake was moving well ahead of me. I peered from under my umbrella and saw that he was now marching, swinging his arms. I made the effort to catch up with him and as I got closer I could hear him chanting, 'Left right left right left right.'

I tried to keep up with him but knew I couldn't sustain it. 'Come on, Kate,' he urged. 'Left right left right.' I grabbed his arm and for a second I thought he was going to hit me but he stopped marching and stood still, head up and shoulders back.

'It's time to go back, Blake. It's lunch time. If we're late we'll be on a charge.'

That line worked. He did an about-turn and was soon marching back with me lagging behind.

As we neared Peace Haven he stopped by a five-bar gate and looked out over the sodden but green countryside. 'British green is the best in the world. Have you noticed how many shades of green there are? It's so fucking beautiful.'

It was a nice view, I agreed, but for me it needed the sunshine to be beautiful.

He wanted to soak up the view. I was merely soaked.

'I've just come back from Iraq,' he began, 'and I can't get things sorted in my head. I have nightmares. There is so much dust and blood and there are flies buzzing in the blood and noise and screaming and babble . . .' He broke off.

I looked at his face. It looked different. He was terrified, but he was no longer in the rain in Wales. In his mind he'd never left Iraq. 'Look, look,' he shouted at a large stone at the side of the path.

'What can you see?' I asked.

'It's a fucking head!' he screamed. 'Can't you see it? There's blood everywhere. It's Pete's head — his head is off. Look, there's his arm.'

I put my umbrella over him and shouted as though trying to deaden the noises in his head. 'Listen, Blake. Listen to the rain. You're in Wales now. Listen!' After a few moments of silence from him I removed the umbrella and let him feel the rain. He stared at the rain as it ran off his hands.

‘It’s not blood,’ he muttered.

I took his hand. ‘Come on, we have to get back.’

‘Yeah,’ he said. ‘Get to safety.’

‘That’s it,’ I encouraged. ‘Let’s run.’

He ran off at speed leaving me trotting behind him like a lame sheep.

Blake was waiting for me with the door open. He was back in Wales. ‘Just in time for lunch,’ he said as though we’d just had a morning constitutional. He wasn’t out of breath but he was soaked through. My lungs were fit to burst and my jeans hung on my legs sodden and cold. He walked towards the dining area and I put my hand out to stop him. ‘You have to get changed first.’

We went to our rooms and I dried my legs with warm towels quickly and put on dry clothes; I was starving. Blake had obviously dressed at the double and was already sitting at the table. Even as I approached the table I felt the atmosphere. Was it because we’d held up lunch? Fran looked the same as ever, wan and sad. Cheryl had been crying and Howard looked tense and troubled. Wayne, still gorgeous but impassive, stared straight ahead.

‘We’ve been for a walk,’ I said, hoping to break the silence.

‘How far did you get?’ asked Howard.

I looked to Blake for an answer. I guessed six miles but guessing distances is one of my many weak points.

Blake muttered, ‘About three miles — it was only a stroll.’

It was my idea of a long hike so I was glad I hadn’t put a figure on the distance.

‘Did you see anyone?’ asked Howard.

‘Not a single soul,’ I said. ‘Just trees and fields and rain.’

‘There was a farm in the distance,’ said Blake, ‘and one of those derelict stone barns.’

I’d seen neither but then I’d been huddled under my umbrella.

‘No cars?’ asked Howard.

Blake shook his head. Howard seemed jittery but then our first course of potato and leek soup arrived and silence reigned again. The hot soup was delicious and although I sneaked the occasional glance at my companions I was feeding my stomach and not my brain. Once on to the main course of a prawn salad I noticed that Howard still seemed tense and had dark rings under his eyes. Fran seemed to be enjoying her salad and Cheryl had begun flirting with Wayne. Once or twice he smiled cheerily.

Then from the kitchen came one almighty clatter. We were all startled but the effect on Blake was startling. He began screaming, 'Get down! Get down! You stupid bastards, get down!' He was already under the table. I got down with him but nothing I could have said would have helped. He was whimpering. I hugged him close and then Zoton appeared and helped us both out from under the table.

As Zoton guided Blake upstairs he said, 'We'll send for a doctor. He'll be fine. Just carry on with your lunch.'

That was easier said than done. The others looked at me as if I should come up with a reason. I merely said, 'Iraq.'

Just one word but it was enough. Fran, who rarely spoke, murmured, 'Poor boy.'

I realized that she was right. Behind the tired eyes, the scruffiness and five o'clock shadow he was the baby of the group, probably in his early twenties, and already he'd seen more horror than most of us would see in a lifetime.

The doctor arrived an hour later — at least his black bag suggested he was a doctor — followed by our body maintenance therapists. Wayne and Howard decided to go the games room, leaving us three women with a choice of a visit to the hairdresser or the beautician, who also gave massage and alternative therapies, or a personal trainer. Cheryl wanted the personal trainer and Fran and I tossed a coin because we kept saying, 'You choose'. I needed all three options but there was plenty of time because the therapists stayed for three hours. I chose heads, which was appropriate because I 'won' the hairdresser.

Her name was Opal, she was young and slim and she had her hair plaited West Indian style. The salon was tiny with one sink, a few shelves full of fluffy white towels, a trolley full of hairdressing gear and my chair facing a huge well-lit mirror.

'How long did your plaits take?' I asked.

'Seven hours or so, but it's low maintenance.'

I was shocked. I'd expect full body cosmetic surgery in that length of time. Conversation wasn't a problem; Opal was a talker. Even while washing my hair she talked. She had West Indian parents who'd come to Wales in the sixties and she'd never even seen the West Indies, which I thought was rather sad. 'I like Wales,' she said in her strong Welsh accent. 'I've got a lovely Welsh boyfriend and I'm getting married next year. We might move to Cardiff; there's lots going on there, clubs and restaurants — it'll be great.'

She paused to wrap a towel around my head. 'Mind you, if we move I'll miss this job. I've been here since the place opened, more than a year now. It takes me a while to get here, I live about fifteen miles away, but they pay for petrol and my time so it doesn't matter.'

As she combed my hair and asked what style I wanted I made a snap decision. 'You decide,' I said. 'But I want something fashionable and young-looking.'

'Right you are,' she said.

With scissors in hand and concentration required she fell silent so I took the opportunity to ask, 'Has there ever been any sort of trouble here?'

'Depends what you mean by trouble,' she said. 'There was a murder just after it opened. One of the counsellors got done in by one of the guests. That's why they had to lose their own names. He'd left here, see, but he found out a home address and he went and set fire to the house. Mad, of course.'

'So most of the guests are OK?' I asked.

'We've had one or two who seemed a bit barmy but mostly it's people who need to escape for a while . . .' She paused. 'Look, I'm saying too much. We're not supposed to talk about the guests. We sign this form, see.' She was frowning now.

'It's not a problem, Opal. You haven't told me a thing. One thing does puzzle me though: this church is miles from anywhere — why?'

'In Wales they like chapels and this church was built in a village for the English. The old people say the English got so fed up with aggravation from the Welsh that they demolished their houses and went back to England.'

'When was this?'

'Hundreds of years ago. When the developers first came a few years back the church was only a shell. It must have cost millions to make it like it is now.'

Opal continued to shape my hair with her scissors in silence and I could only try to work out the cost of renovation, of utilities, of furnishings, of food and last but not least the cost of staff for a mere six guests. The question remained: why? Someone must be subsidising the whole outfit.

'Has anyone really famous ever been here?'

'Oh, yes. There was that MP that was having death threats. They told a lot of lies about him in the newspapers. They said he was killed in a hit-and-run accident in Essex but we know he was found in a field not far from here, shot right through the heart.'

'Didn't everyone know? Wasn't there a fuss locally?'

She shook her head. 'It was very hush-hush. You see they paid the staff to keep quiet. So we did.'

Opal seemed to think being bribed was perfectly normal and somehow I thought the amounts paid out would be quite substantial. Everyone has a price, I supposed, but it was still worrying.

As Opal finished my hair I was a little surprised at my shaggy new look but admitted it made me look a little trendier. But my hair wasn't as important as finding out who ran this organisation and why. I told myself there was no need to know but my suspicions had been aroused. The place felt sinister; why the blackout on news? Was there something that Peace Haven didn't want us to know? If an MP was involved, was the government itself using the place for some reason?

CHAPTER SIX

Opal showed me the back of my hair in a mirror and I tried one last ploy.

'Do you have a mobile phone?' I asked casually.

'That's my lifeline,' she said, giving my hair a final lift with the end of her comb. 'I couldn't manage without one.'

'Nor me. I'm desperate to get in touch with my boyfriend. We can use the phone here but it's not the same.'

'I know what you mean,' she said with a big smile. 'I always talk to my boyfriend from my bed. There's no signal here but if you walk about a mile to Davies Point you can get a signal there.'

'Which way?'

'Turn left, keep going up the lane and you'll see a little hill and an old barn. If you stand on that hill you can get a signal.'

I gave her the emergency ten pounds I kept in my bra, which was the only good piece of advice my mother had ever given me. Her smile grew broader and I walked out with a new hair style and a new purpose.

On the ground floor Howard was in the lounge slumped on a sofa staring into space. He looked up and smiled. 'You look great,' he said.

'Thanks. Where's Wayne? I thought you two were playing table tennis.'

'He's gone to the gym room. I'm waiting for a massage.'

I sat down on the sofa next to him. 'What do you think of this place, Howard?'

'It's OK.'

'Don't you think the whole set up is odd?'

He shrugged. 'It's modern and a bit new age, but I needed a break.'

'Why?' I asked bluntly.

'You're asking too many questions, Kate. Let's just say if I wasn't here I'd have to be in a psychiatric hospital.'

'We all seem in that condition.'

He stared at me until I began to feel uncomfortable. 'You look OK to me,' he said. His tone was nasty now. 'I reckon,' he said, 'you're the odd one out here.'

I changed the subject. 'Is there any news on Blake?'

'He's asleep. Rogon thinks he'll be down for supper.'

'Good.'

A door above us closed and soft footsteps heralded the arrival of Fran. She was smiling and looked refreshed. 'The massage was absolutely wonderful,' she said.

Howard stood up. 'It's my turn then. See you.'

Now that I was alone with Fran she picked up a copy of *Good Housekeeping* magazine and began flicking through the pages. 'Your hair looks really good,' she murmured.

I thanked her and waited a few moments before asking, 'Are you enjoying it here?'

She paused so long before answering she was either undecided or she didn't want to talk at all. 'It's OK. I'm adaptable.'

She really was hard work but I wanted to talk. So I tried again. 'Do you know who funded this place originally?'

She didn't even look up from her magazine. 'No. Why should I? Does it matter? It's expensive enough. I should think it makes a profit.'

'Who reaps the benefits then?'

'I don't know and I don't care.'

I was on the wrong tack. I tried another one. 'I expect you miss your family. I'm missing my home and my dog Jasper.'

'I don't have a family. There's no one,' she said, still without looking up.

I do know when to give up so I muttered, 'See you later.' She didn't respond.

I walked from the lounge to the main body of the building. Perhaps it had once been the aisle but now it was wide and empty and as silent as the old tombs outside. I did see Dave scurrying off when he saw me, or perhaps he was just in a hurry. He seemed to be going towards the kitchen. I glanced sideways and saw he'd left his office door ajar. I was in as fast as a whippet and knew exactly what I was looking for. In the cushion under the chair I found it — a copy of the *Sun*. It was a week old but I didn't care. I stuffed the newspaper up my jumper under my left arm and made a guilty but quick exit.

In my room I went straight to the bathroom and hid the newspaper under my clean towels. The room had obviously been entered because the towels were fresh and there were extra tea bags on the tray. Someone must have been in whilst I was trekking with Blake. So far I hadn't seen a cleaner or a chamber maid.

Why I wanted to save my precious newspaper until later I didn't know but something denied is always a treasure — and just maybe there was a reason why Dave had kept a week-old copy of the *Sun*.

I returned to the lounge feeling a little sense of triumph. Fran was still there but she didn't look up as I approached. I too picked up a copy of *Good Housekeeping*. It was six months old, so in contrast my *Sun* was a real find.

Wayne joined us twenty silent minutes later. 'I'm out of condition,' he complained. He was sweating a little but his spirits seemed to have lifted. 'The trainer suggests I have a short run each morning. Is anyone up for it?'

'I'll come,' I said, 'but I trot, I don't run.'

'That's fine. It's still good for you.'

Later on that afternoon I had a wonderful massage with various different oils and I was so relaxed I couldn't chat to Wendy, the young masseuse. Wearing only my knickers — medium-sized lacy ones — and covered by warm towels I began to drift off, still trying to make sense of my surroundings. My companions were a mysterious group; only Blake and Cheryl's problems were obvious. They could both be suffering from post-traumatic stress disorder — were we all to some degree suffering or suspected of suffering from it? Were the kaftan brigade really social scientists working on some university research project? And were we mere guinea pigs? If so, perhaps as part of the experiment I was a control of one among six.

The massage continued and I could think no more. I allowed Wendy's gentle hands to soothe all my negative suspicious thoughts away. When she finally told me the massage was over and that I could sit up slowly I did feel wonderfully relaxed and refreshed but also disappointed that it was over.

* * *

Back in my room I lay on the bed for a while staring at the ceiling and telling myself that I didn't need to make friends, create a mystery where there was none or indeed invent conspiracy theories. I was here to improve my mental health. I should be grateful for good food and pampering. I counted a few more blessings — which if you need sleep works better than counting sheep — and soon my eyes closed. I had wanted to read my newspaper but that could wait for it only contained gossip, celebrity bashing and bad news.

The gong woke me. I was horrified. I'd wanted to change my clothes but food came first so I raked a brush through my hair and a quick glance in the mirror showed that my neat but spiky hair cut was now merely spiky. I shrugged mentally. Who cared but me?

I was the last at the table. Even Blake had made it on time. He looked pale and spaced out but I guessed he'd been given some tranquilisers. He managed a smile. Cheryl sat next to Wayne and I had a feeling they were playing footsie under the table.

It was Rogon that served us. She spoke to everyone as she handed round the plates. She even told me my hair looked nice and asked how I'd enjoyed the massage. 'I manage to sneak one in occasionally,' she said, 'if Wendy isn't busy.'

Fran managed to smile at me and Howard, who sat on my right, whispered, 'I reckon Rogon wasn't born but was developed under a mushroom — an alien life force.'

It was obvious that Rogon was making an effort but had she been told to? What on earth did Argon and Zoton do all day? I supposed that if Argon's job was equated with a hotel manager guests would only want him to be available, not ever-present. My suspicion, and I couldn't get rid of it, was that we were being watched every minute of the day and possibly the night. They were working in shifts — one sleeping, one watching and one available. I would have loved to see inside the new extension where they had their quarters. The out-of-bounds kitchen, I was fairly sure, led to their lair.

'Kate — any dessert for you?' asked Rogon. 'There's a choice of . . .' She broke off as Blake, who sat opposite me, began drumming on the table with his fork.

We all stopped and stared but he was oblivious to us. 'Get him!' he began shouting. 'Get him!'

'It's all right, mate,' said Howard. 'You calm down. We've got him now.'

Blake didn't hear. 'Do as I bloody say,' he shouted. 'Get the bastard.' He put down the fork and picked up the knife and began jabbing the air. We were both shocked and mesmerized. None of us, including Rogon, knew quite what to do. The arrival of Argon and Zoton went unnoticed as Blake stood up and began stabbing the table. 'Kill the fucker,' he screamed. 'Kill him!'

So-called counsellors Argon and Zoton didn't bother with words. They grabbed his arms, put him in an arm lock and began the struggle to remove him. Blake kicked out, swearing and cursing. 'Don't let the bastard live,' he shouted. 'I'll get him. I'll get the murdering bastard.' Blake was dragged away with Rogon following, trying to avoid his feet as they kicked out. We watched as Blake was taken to his room. We could still hear him shouting for several minutes afterwards.

No one knew what to say. Fran looked close to tears, half stood up, and then sat down again. It was Howard who broke the shocked silence. 'I'm having dessert,' he said. 'Shame to waste it.'

'I need a drink,' wailed Cheryl. Wayne whispered something in her ear and a few minutes later they left the table and headed upstairs.

Howard winked at me. 'That will do her more good than a bottle of vodka.'

I suppose he was trying to lift our downcast mood but it didn't work. We drank our coffee in silence. Fran, still near to tears, suddenly said, 'Alcohol never solves anything. It's a blight on family life, on society, on everything damn thing.'

'Everything in moderation, my darling,' said Howard.

'That's what I thought,' she said bitterly. 'I thought I drank in moderation. But you sit there, smug and self-satisfied, and make stupid remarks — bitchy, snide little asides, I've heard you.'

'Whoa there, lady. There's no need to lose your rag because you've got a drink problem. Shit happens.'

'Tragedies happen. Terrible deeds through people being drunk . . .'

'I've had enough of this,' said Howard. 'I'm going to flounce off to my room.'

And so he did.

Fran looked at me with tears in her eyes and was about to say more when the bell at the front door rang. We exchanged glances as if deciding which of us should answer it but by then Rogon had rushed down the stairs. The man she took up to Blake's room carried a black bag, so again we presumed he was a doctor. We looked up towards the bedrooms and saw Wayne and Cheryl wearing jackets and creeping out. Cheryl stood at the balustrade, looked down on us and put her index finger to her lips.

'So much for Howard's theory,' said Fran. 'Although I suppose they had time for a quickie.' That was the first comment Fran had made to show that beneath her sad exterior there was a once happy woman with a sense of humour. Somehow she didn't fit my preconceptions of an alcoholic but I was often wrong and even drug addicts manage to hide their condition and lead normal lives.

We heard Wayne and Cheryl close the front door. They were probably sneaking out to the local pub if they could find one. There was no street lighting and the narrow lanes stretched for miles, but after all we weren't prisoners, even though the atmosphere of the place suggested that we were.

Fran sighed and sat back in her chair. 'I don't feel like going to bed yet. I'm not used to the quiet.'

That seemed an odd comment but I didn't feel tired either so we sat for a while in silence. Then Fran abruptly said, 'Why are you here, Kate?'

'It was organized for me,' I said with an attempt at a smile. 'Supposedly to cure my depression.'

'You're not running from anyone then?'

'Only myself.'

'Why?'

I shrugged, not really wanting to talk about David's death, and yet it was always with me. 'I found my boyfriend in his car. I thought he was alive. He wasn't. He was dead, murdered — colder than a marble floor.'

'Were you in love with him?'

'No, but who knows, one day I could have been. He wanted to marry me.'

Fran smiled. 'It could have been a lucky escape. In my experience marriage can be fraught and miserable.'

'Do you have any plans after you leave here?' I asked, wanting to look forwards and not back.

'My friend has found me somewhere to live but I have to earn a living and professionally I'm persona non grata.'

I didn't want to pry so I told her I sometimes dreamt of glamorous jobs in public relations or fashion design or being an estate agent in Bermuda.

She smiled. 'Nothing too useful then?'

'No. But it won't happen. It's as likely as winning the lottery.'

'I'd like to run my own business but I don't know what's safe and likely to make money.'

'Can you cook? Foodies are always looking for someone to cook for their up-market dinner parties.'

She shook her head. 'I'm only a basic cook and to be honest I don't have that much interest in food.'

'What about taking courses in new age stuff like reflexology and Indian head massage?'

Again she shook her head. 'I'm too down to earth and I'm not sure I want to work with people. I just want . . . peace.'

I knew exactly what she meant and we chatted for a while, although I did most of the talking, bemoaning my lack of girlfriends and girly nights out. When we decided to go to bed we were in agreement that we both needed more fun in our lives but what to do about it remained a mystery.

Reality kicked in as we passed Blake's room and heard low voices. 'He should be in hospital,' I said, thinking aloud.

'Thanks for the chat,' said Fran as we went to our rooms.

In the bathroom I retrieved my stolen copy of the *Sun* and perched on the bed to read it. Having had a long nap in the afternoon I worried now that I wouldn't be able to sleep. At that moment I really missed talking to Hubert but I resolved to find Davies Point in the morning and then make it a regular calling spot.

Then I saw it, on the inside of the front page, just a few telling lines and a fuzzy photo:

> *Former divorce lawyer Francesca Rowley, aged 38, is to be freed early. The stony-faced baby killer who showed no remorse for her crime has served the last months of her*

sentence in cushy Bancroft open prison. A small group were gathering outside the prison today to protest.

I read it twice. I looked at the photo several times. I was pretty certain it was Fran.

Was she stony-faced? She had high cheek bones and with a little help her eyes would have been stunning. Her mouth was often set but when she did smile it transformed her.

I decided it was none of my business and thinking about her would stop me sleeping, so I tried to do the crosswords and the puzzles but I couldn't concentrate. I wanted to know the full story. What drove a professional woman to kill a baby? I'd not read about her before; maybe I'd been away at the time. I was pretty sure Hubert would have heard of the case and I longed to talk to him but it would have to wait for now.

I took a long hot bath and at ten thirty I went to bed and tried to sleep. It was like being in a race; I was in front and the finishing line was sleep then I slipped back with troubled thoughts zapping into my mind at random. The finishing line just got further and further away.

At just after one o'clock I thought I heard a door open and footsteps but I dozed off and then I had a nightmare in which someone was screaming. I sat bolt upright.

It was no dream. Someone *was* screaming, lights were going on, footsteps sounded, doors banging — panic.

I grabbed my dressing gown and rushed from my room barefoot.

CHAPTER SEVEN

It was Cheryl who was screaming hysterically. Wayne looked upwards in horror. It took me a moment to realize what was happening. Blake was hanging from the topmost balustrade. Below, Dave was struggling with a ladder. Zoton, in a red dressing gown, was standing by the rope looking down. Then I saw Fran, white-faced, standing by her bedroom door retching violently. Argon helped Dave set up the ladder. Then he shouted, 'There's nothing anyone can do. Everyone go back to your rooms — now!'

I helped Fran into her bathroom where she was violently sick. I concentrated on looking after her but my knees wobbled and I could feel my heart racing. She refused to lie down in bed but agreed to sit up if I promised not to leave her. She gripped my hand so hard that I couldn't leave without a struggle anyway. After a few minutes she relaxed her grip a little then she took several deep breaths and became more composed. Her face, still pale and shadowy in the light of the bedside lamp, looked hard. Her mouth was set as if she were clenching her teeth. The phrase 'she showed no remorse' sprang into my mind.

'You know, don't you?' she said miserably. I nodded, surprised my expression had been so obvious. 'I can't stay here,' she said. 'The police will come, we'll all be interviewed. I can't go through it again. I'm leaving.' The words were said calmly enough but she still held on to my hand.

'It won't be a murder enquiry,' I said. 'We know Blake was disturbed.'

'They still have to take statements,' she murmured. 'I thought I'd be safe here. They promised . . .' She broke off.

'Who promised?'

'It doesn't matter. I'm leaving here as soon as I can.'

'We can't go anywhere at the moment. Shall I make some tea?'

We drank tea and we both relaxed a little. I refused to think about what was going on downstairs and sensed that Fran wanted to talk. I'd learnt my lesson though. I let her lead the conversation.

'Have you got a sister?' she asked.

'No. Just a globe-trotting wayward mother.'

'My sister and I were very close once. We had a single mum. She qualified as a teacher after my father walked out on us. She worked so hard, she even worked in the school holidays. That left Claudette and me together most of the time. We worked hard too. Our mother, Carol, drummed it into our heads that we had to get professional qualifications before we got married and that saving money was virtually an instruction from God.'

'Did it work?'

'Not really. Claudette rebelled at sixteen, left school, worked in a bank and married a rich older man when she was twenty. He bought her a car, a grand house and set up a bank account for her . . .' She paused. 'She is of course absolutely stunning. She had the looks and I had the ambition.'

'But you were successful?'

'I qualified as a solicitor, married in my traineeship and a landed a job with Hunter, Hunter and Blaze, mostly working in family liaison — trying to make sure any children got the best deal possible.'

Even I had heard of that firm. The rich and famous went there for their divorces, especially celebrity women who wanted huge settlements and usually won.

'It sounds interesting and worthwhile.'

Fran stared at me. 'At first it was. My husband — ex-husband now — Neil worked long hours in a high-flying job in an accountancy firm. So we more or less arrived home together. I could cope with the stress. We bought a four-bedroomed house in Belsize Park — with a mortgage, of course. We had a very good lifestyle.'

'What went wrong?'

She tried to smile. 'I got pregnant. Next day Neil informed me he had resigned from his job so that he could work at home.'

'That doesn't sound so bad. It works for lots of families.'

'Maybe. But he wanted to paint. He thought he was a genius. He had no talent whatsoever. He took out a second mortgage so that he could convert the attic into a studio. He bought the best of everything. Money just slipped through his fingers. I carried on working until a week before Fiona was born. We usually called her Fifi. She was beautiful . . .' Fran squared her shoulders and took a deep breath. I sat wondering if Fiona was the baby she'd killed. 'Neil was as besotted as I was. I stayed away from work for six weeks although they sent files to my house and rang me several times a day. In some ways it was a relief to leave Fifi in Neil's capable hands and go back to the office. The backlog of work was horrendous. My boss blamed me for being too popular as clients were willing to wait for me to return.'

I refilled our cups from the teapot and although I heard movement downstairs, Fran didn't notice. Blake's death seemed to have allowed her to open up; perhaps fear and death is eased by talking about life.

'I'm talking too much,' she said.

'No, you're not. I'm interested.'

'Why?'

'Because I'm nosey.'

'At least you're honest.'

The ship's bell at the front door distracted us both. Fran paled. 'Oh my God, that's the police.'

I opened the door and peered over the balustrade; there was no sign of Blake's body and Argon was already at the door. The two burly men who entered walked straight towards the stairs. I dashed back and kept the door open a fraction. Just before they passed Fran's room I closed the door.

'They are not the police, Fran,' I told her. 'They're Red Caps, MPs — military police.'

'I expect they have to come first,' said Fran as she moved from the bed and came over to the door. We waited for several minutes hearing nothing so I opened the door wider and we both looked down on the scene. There was no one to be seen. I'm sure that Fran shared my thoughts. The body shouldn't have been removed until a police surgeon had estimated time and cause of death. I'd heard once of a murder where a man was strangled manually and then his body hung from a roof joist. Finger marks on the neck gave the murderer away, of course.

'What's going on?' asked Fran.

I had no idea but it made me uneasy. A man's life had ended and it seemed as if the army didn't have to follow the rules.

As we stood there waiting for something to happen, the ship's bell rang. Dave answered the door and two men in black suits entered carrying a coffin draped with a purple cover. This time we both stood in the doorway. The two Red Caps hurried down the stairs and two minutes later the undertakers brought down Blake's body. I bowed my head. Fran crossed herself.

We closed the door and sat on the bed again. I looked at my watch — it was two thirty a.m. A man, a soldier with no surname, had died and been removed within the hour. It seemed indecent haste. Older nurses I'd spoken to who'd nursed in the sixties had told me that one peaceful hour was needed after death so that the spirit could leave the body.

Not so in hospitals today. Poor Blake had died and had already been dispatched. A sadness fell over me and I not only wanted a drink, I needed one.

As if reading my mind Fran said, 'I've got a small bottle of vodka hidden. Someone gave it to me, a sick joke I think, because I'll never drink again.'

'I wouldn't tempt you by opening it,' I said. 'It just wouldn't be fair.'

We fell silent; the earlier sense of intimacy had gone. I really wanted to know what had gone wrong with her life but I didn't want to pry. I sensed that when she was ready she'd tell me.

The silence was abruptly broken when she asked, 'What do you do for a living, Kate?'

I hesitated. What was the point of lying? 'I'm a private investigator.'

'Are you any good?'

'All I can say is that I've managed to pay the rent for a few years. I get quite a lot of help from my landlord, Hubert. He's an undertaker.'

'Are you an item?'

I smiled. 'No. He's a lot older than me, not very attractive, but . . .' I broke off, not sure how I did feel.

'You love him,' she said with certainty. 'I used to meet couples who were angry, upset and uncertain about loving each other. Normal life is a real passion killer and some people can't cope with that. They look for passion elsewhere and then find that too slips away.'

'Is that what happened to you and Neil?'

'His passion was his art, and the children of course, but even that wasn't enough. He started seeing other women, going to casinos and nightclubs. I hoped it was a phase that would pass. To some extent it did. When Fiona was three I gave birth to Benjamin. Neil had promised me he'd change and he dearly wanted a son. He'd sold a couple of his paintings to rich friends who wouldn't know a Matisse from a

Turner but that paid for his car and helped towards the cost of a nanny so that he'd be free to paint during the day.'

Tiredness began to creep over me. I yawned twice in a row and Fran took the hint.

'You go to bed, Kate. I'm fine now — really.'

Back in my room and in bed, sleep didn't come that easily. I thought first of Blake. Had he packed the rope in his luggage, planning it way in advance, or had he acquired the rope at Peace Haven? Did our counsellors know in advance he had suicidal thoughts and was generally disturbed? Was he on medication? There were so many questions but I had a feeling that Argon and his cohorts would scarcely mention him again.

As for Fran, whilst I could perhaps see her being driven to kill her husband in a jealous rage, I simply couldn't imagine her killing her own child. She seemed to be a self-disciplined person whose ambition wasn't that overwhelming. But the demon drink did seem to have played some part in the tragedy. Eventually I gave up supposition and dozed off.

It seemed only minutes later that the gong sounded for breakfast. Zombie-like I splashed my face with cold water, brushed my teeth and got dressed. I thought I'd be the last down but only Howard and I arrived at the same time.

We sat together and drank strong coffee waiting for the others to arrive. Howard seemed depressed. 'Bloody shame about Blake,' he said. 'Expedient, I suppose.'

'What's that supposed to mean?'

'For the army, I meant.'

'Could you explain?'

He shrugged. 'No harm in telling you now, I suppose. Blake should have been court-martialled for murder but because of his mental state and the death threats they sent him here instead — hoping, I suppose, he'd be fit enough to plead — or simply to keep it out of the press.'

I stared at him. 'Why are you here, Howard?'

'Oh, sweetheart,' he said, shaking his head. 'You haven't got a clue, have you?'

‘What are you trying to say?’ I asked irritably.

‘I’m trying to tell you that this place is a safe house, meaning witness protection or protection in general.’

‘There’s been a mistake then,’ I said. ‘I’m just here because I’ve been a bit depressed.’

He shrugged. ‘Think about it, love. You’re here for the same reason we’re all here. Our lives are in danger.’

CHAPTER EIGHT

Howard poured me another cup of coffee. I needed it. 'There's been a mistake in my case,' I said. 'How could I be in any sort of danger and not know it?'

He shrugged. 'I've no idea. Do you open all your post? See all your e-mails? Answer every phone call?'

I was about to say of course I did. But that wasn't true. The post came in a batch, the last few weeks Hubert had checked my e-mails and the land line phone was always ringing. Surely Hubert would have told me though? But then it shouldn't come as a surprise that Hubert might have been trying to protect me and that this place wasn't simply found on the internet. He'd lied to me. But who on earth would want me dead?

Howard stared at me intently for several seconds. 'Have you any idea how the witness scheme works?' I shook my head. 'Well, sweetheart,' he said. 'Would it surprise you to know that there is a small town in England with five families under the scheme?' I was surprised, of course. 'Once your identity is changed,' Howard told me, 'you lose everything, your friends, family members, old haunts, your home, your job. Effectively, you've died.'

'I'd never thought of it like that.'

'Some people deserve it, but most don't. There's one compensation,' he said.

'What's that?'

'You get the chance to see a shrink once a month,' he said bitterly.

The arrival of Wayne, Cheryl and Fran stopped our conversation but not my anxiety. As if on cue Argon also appeared. He stood at the head of the table and said solemnly, 'Last night's events were tragic. Please rest assured that Blake did kill himself. He left a detailed suicide note.' His glance fell on Cheryl and Wayne. 'If you wish to leave the premises for whatever reason please inform us where you going and what time you expect to be back. This is for your own protection. We would of course prefer you not to leave the premises, or at least to stay within a short radius. After breakfast please go to your One to One rooms.'

He didn't wait for questions as he swept away with his over-long kaftan trailing on the floor.

'Well, that's told us,' said Wayne. 'Did you notice there wasn't a word of regret about Blake's death?'

There was a murmur of agreement. Fran caught my eye. 'Shall we do our one to one now?' I nodded and we excused ourselves.

The pass-the-parcel box sat there on the desk but neither of us wanted to participate in that particular activity. I wanted to find out how much Fran knew about the place and who exactly was running it. When we'd sat down I blurted out, 'Did *you* know this place was a safe house?'

'Yes, of course, didn't you?'

'No. I didn't know I was under any threat.'

'Lucky you,' she said. 'Shall I tell you about the others?'

'You know about them?' I asked, surprised.

'Even in prison we had newspapers — and they *have* talked to me.'

This time I showed no surprise. Fran was the quiet, receptive type that would let someone talk without interruption.

'How did you find about me then?'

'Just from a few lines in a week-old copy of the *Sun*.'

'I will tell you more later on,' she said. 'In the meantime I'll tell you about Cheryl. This is what she's told me and it isn't a secret. As she says, we're all in the same boat.'

Fran sat herself forward and crossed her hands as if to keep them still. 'Cheryl is in hiding from career criminals. Her husband, Kyle Himley, was thought to be the mastermind behind the Fitzroy bank raid six years before. Only there was no proof and he had an alibi in Cheryl and her best friend. Three-in-a-bed sex at the time of the robbery was a good enough alibi so he got away with it. Or so it seemed for some time until the gang fell out over the distribution, and whereabouts of the bulk of the cash. They targeted Cheryl for information, slashed her with razors and knives and threatened to cut her breasts off.'

'She told me her husband had done that,' I said, shocked.

'It wasn't him. She says she has no idea where the money is hidden so she wasn't being either stupid or brave. Together they hatched a plot to convince the police that Kyle had attacked her because she'd taunted him about other men. His barrister guessed rightly that the judge might be somewhat sympathetic. He sent him down for seven years. With good behaviour he would be out in four years and then able to find new allies and be relatively safe. Cheryl went abroad for a while but she's back and hoping for her share of the loot. Kyle is due out now and the police fear Cheryl will be either killed or kidnapped just to get back at Kyle.'

At the moment it seemed to me that Cheryl was more than keen on Wayne but perhaps she was clinging on to him as a protector and if she had to feign passion that was the price to be paid. Who was I kidding? He was drop-dead gorgeous. She didn't have to feign anything.

'What happens when she leaves here?'

'It seems the police have done some sort of deal with Kyle. He'll turn informant and forgo most of the money in exchange for witness protection.'

'How do you think Kyle will react if he finds out about Wayne?'

She smiled wryly. 'As they say in the trade — he'd go ballistic. He'd kill her, that's for sure.'

That was a chilling thought. Although Cheryl was a good liar, could she keep quiet?

'I'd love to go out for a walk now,' said Fran wistfully. 'There's no countryside in prison.'

'You're on,' I said. 'I need to make a phone call from Davies Point. It seems it's the nearest place around here to get a mobile signal.'

We looked at the pass-the-parcel box in unison. 'There's no point in doing it now,' she said. 'They're watching our every move.'

I wasn't surprised but to have my suspicions confirmed made me very uncomfortable.

'Who told you?'

'Howard.'

I was puzzled. Fran was easily the quietest in our group and yet she knew far more than me. 'I didn't see you talking to him much,' I said.

'I haven't since we arrived,' she explained. 'We travelled to pick-up points near London and a people carrier bought us here. Everyone talked a lot until we got here. I didn't give many details about myself . . .' She broke off. 'Shall we go?'

* * *

Argon raised a warning finger as he opened the front door for us. 'Don't walk too far and be back by lunchtime.' I felt like a schoolgirl but supposed Fran had got used to petty restrictions and following orders.

Outside the sun was breaking through. The air was chilly but there was no wind and the day held a promise of a little spring warmth. 'Isn't it beautiful?' said Fran as we left the church grounds and saw the green vistas ahead. I had to agree; the greenery and the distant hills with the addition of sun seemed magical. Fran being so entranced made me realize how much I took the countryside for granted.

We walked in silence for about half a mile. In the distance we could see the one farmhouse and the derelict stone barn. Today I saw a few sheep but not a human being.

'When I've done the things I have to do,' said Fran quietly, 'I'd like to live here.'

'It's a bit too isolated for me. I'd feel lonely.'

'I was lonely in prison surrounded by other people. Being really alone means you have no expectations. You have to make the best of it.'

'Is that what life is really about?' I said. 'Just making the best of it?'

'I think that now. For the first year I just wanted to die. I was given anti-depressants until I was numb. I couldn't feel the pain any more but the absence of pain didn't make me feel better.'

'Tell me about it,' I urged her. 'I'm being nosey as usual but sometimes it does help to talk.'

She stopped and stared into the distance. 'It might depress you. And you'll despise me.'

We walked on and the sun shone a little brighter. Suddenly Fran said, 'I have to find my son's grave.'

'Where is he buried?'

'I don't know. No one wants me to know. Not my ex-husband, my sister, or my so-called friends — no one wants me to know.'

'Why not?'

'Because I killed him, of course.'

That statement was a real conversation stopper. But she *was* talking and it seemed she needed to. I had to remind myself that this wasn't a 'case'; I had no need to know any more. 'Do you want to tell me about it?' I asked but in some ways I hoped she didn't. Peace Haven was mystery enough for me.

We rounded a sharp bend in the narrow lane and there, a short distance away, was Davies Point. Hubert and Jasper dominated my thoughts now. I felt as if I'd been away from them for a very long time. I supposed that was a combination of having distanced myself since David's death and now being physically away from them. I hurried towards the hill, although it was more a mound than a hill. Once on top of it I took out my mobile phone and crossed my fingers that there would be a signal and that Hubert would be able to speak to me. His message system kicked in almost immediately. I wasn't prepared to leave a message. I'd decided to wait on Davies Point until he answered.

Fran sat down on the grass hugging her knees. 'Your friend Hubert would know how to find a grave, wouldn't he?' she asked.

'I suppose he would if it was in the UK. Where's your ex-husband living?'

She shrugged. 'I've no idea.'

'Your sister?'

'She moved after my arrest. There was media interest in her too. You know the sort of thing: *Baby killer's sister tells all.*'

'And did she tell all?'

'Yes, with embellishments, but after I was convicted of course.'

That seemed to me like the ultimate betrayal but there was no trace of bitterness in her voice. 'She did it for the money?' I asked.

'Yes. If my little sister could marry for money then she could easily sell her sister. The press hated me before but after her so-called revelations they were relentless.'

'Are you here because of the media?'

'Yes, but also because of the death threats.'

'Even in prison?' I asked surprised.

'Oh, yes. I was attacked several times. I was a prime target as the rich bitch that couldn't keep her man and killed her son to get back at him.'

I hesitated. 'Was there any truth in that?'

Fran stared ahead for a few moments. Then she turned and looked at me with her sad eyes. 'I don't know what the truth is any more. Perhaps I am the wicked person most people think I am.'

'You must have some supporters?'

She nodded. 'A colleague at Hunters acted as my solicitor and found me a barrister. He's been my only prison visitor over the years. He's been really kind and offered to help me find somewhere to live, but before that I want to see Benjamin's grave and try to find out where Fiona is. My heart is aching to see her again if only briefly. She'll be eleven now . . .' She broke off. 'I can't talk about this any more. I'm sorry. You make your phone call. I'll on walk a bit more.'

Hubert answered the phone this time. After the usual pleasantries, mostly about Jasper who wasn't pining and Hubert who said he was, I ventured a suggestion that Hubert had told me a porkie pie about finding Peace Haven on the internet.

'You've found me out,' he said. 'I had a feeling you would.'

'So why am I here? Have there been any death threats? Am I in any danger?'

'Of course you're not!' He sounded peeved. 'If you must know I arranged your stay at Peace Haven via a police source. There was a spare place and the police paid the bill as a sort of compensation for David's death. After all, if you'd been married to him you'd have received a widow's pension.'

'You're getting very devious,' I said. 'You gave me the impression you'd paid the fees.'

Silence from the other end.

'Did you know Peace Haven is a safe house full of deviant characters?' I asked.

'I didn't know that. Are you OK?'

'I'm fine but one of the guests has committed suicide. He hanged himself.'

It took a moment for that to register. When it did he said, 'I'll come and collect you today.'

'No, don't do that,' I said hurriedly. 'At the moment we all need to stick together and I am genuinely feeling better. I'm counting my blessings and you're still one of them.'

'You know how to butter me up, Kate.'

'I do need a favour.'

'What are you up to? You're not working, are you?'

‘No, of course not, but I need you to find a grave for me — Benjamin Rowley, aged two years. He died approximately six years ago.’

‘I don’t like the sound of this at all. Don’t get involved.’

‘I am involved . . . please . . . please.’

‘Don’t try to soft soap me,’ he said. He paused. ‘You know it works. I’ll do my best.’

‘Kate! Kate!’ Fran was shouting and running towards me. ‘I have to go, thanks Hubert.’

I ran down Davies Point to join Fran who, breathless and agitated, blurted out, ‘There’s a car, two men driving towards Peace Haven.’

‘They could be going to the farm,’ I suggested.

‘I don’t think so. I only got a glimpse but they looked like thugs to me.’

‘I’ll warn Argon,’ I said, fetching out my mobile phone. ‘What’s the number?’

Fran shook her head. ‘It’s OK, we’ll run. No problem.’

We ran as fast as we could and Fran, being slim as a whippet, was soon ahead of me. I ran as fast as my legs would allow; Fran proved to be a sprinter and soon tired. She slowed to my pace and soon we were in the narrow lane that led to Peace Haven. We passed the farm but we didn’t see a car, only a four-wheel-drive.

At Peace Haven, all nervous energy spent, we searched around the immediate grounds. ‘Why are there no cars here anyway?’ I asked, feeling a certain sense of anti-climax.

‘Bombs,’ said Fran. ‘There’s always the danger of car bombs.’

I rang the ship’s bell vigorously. It was Zoton who answered the door. When I told him about the car I noticed he made a well-rehearsed gesture. He felt for his gun.

CHAPTER NINE

I flashed a glance at Fran but she didn't seem to notice. Beneath that kaftan I supposed he could have been hiding a Kalashnikov rifle.

'You won't need your gun,' I said. 'The car must have gone past; we've already had a look round.'

'We'll do the looking,' he said nastily. 'You two go and get some coffee and stay together. No one is to go outside again until we're sure it's safe.'

'How did you know he had gun?' whispered Fran as we walked into the lounge area where the others were sprawled on the sofas.

'Just a flash of intuition,' I said, hoping to impress. In fact his quick response combined with the slightest of bulges at waist level had been enough to convince me.

Moments later Argon and Rogon rushed down the stairs towards the front door.

'What's going on?' asked Howard.

'We saw a car,' said Fran. 'Or at least I did.'

'What make?' snapped Howard.

She thought for a moment. 'I don't know. It was silver with four doors.'

'What about the occupants?'

'It was only the slightest glimpse — two burly men.'

'Black? White?'

'White,' she murmured, staring at Howard. 'You're a cop, aren't you?'

There was only a short pause before he said, 'Sussed again.'

'You're a bloody good actor,' said Wayne admiringly.

'I have to be. I've been working undercover.'

I tried not to show my surprise. Was Howard really gay or just being as camp as possible in the line of duty?

'And before anyone says anything,' said Howard, 'yes, I am gay. But undercover I can be as butch as anyone else.'

Perhaps I'd been a little prejudiced, influenced by films where undercover cops were always macho and even the women were aggressive and fearless. Somehow calling himself Howard the Coward had set the seal on how we perceived him.

'I'll go and have a look round outside,' he said. I noticed that he went in the direction of the kitchen.

The remaining four of us sat down wondering what we should be doing. The strained silence was broken by Cheryl. 'There's no way they could get in here . . . is there?' Her voice betrayed her panic and Wayne immediately put an arm around her shoulder but this time she shrugged him off.

'It could be that the two thugs are after me,' he said. 'So don't worry.'

Cheryl looked anxiously at the two of us. 'You won't say anything, will you? If Kyle finds out he'll kill me.'

'He won't, baby. I'll look after you,' said Wayne, affecting an American southern drawl.

'You can take that smug look off your face,' she snapped. 'He'll kill me quickly. Yours will be a slow and painful death.'

The smug look did indeed leave Wayne's handsome face. 'I can't handle this,' he said. 'I'm leaving. I'll take my chances with my own personal nutter.'

He stood up to leave and now Cheryl looked distraught. 'Don't leave me here. Let's go together, darling . . . please.'

'Oh, no!' he said adamantly. 'I'd *really* be a target then.'

As Wayne walked away she followed him upstairs and we watched as he tried and failed to get into his room without her.

A few minutes later Howard reappeared, apparently having discovered nothing amiss outside.

'Who's after Wayne?' I asked.

'Sad story,' said Howard. 'Wayne was driving home one night after being in a theatre production. It was just after midnight and the pubs and clubs were emptying and there was a crowd of young people, mostly drunk. Two girls were messing about on the kerbside just as Wayne approached. He was not speeding and he hadn't been drinking but the roads were icy. One of the girls walked into the road laughing, throwing her arms about and the other one attempted to grab her. Unfortunately Wayne tried to brake, skidded a bit and hit the girl who was trying to haul back her friend from the road.'

'She was killed?' I asked.

'Not immediately. Wayne was in shock but later that night he went to the hospital to find out how she was . . .' He paused. 'It seems the girl's father blamed Wayne. He went berserk, made all sorts of threats and the threats have continued. At first the police were sympathetic towards the father but then they checked his criminal record. He'd been in prison twice for GBH and once for taking money with menace.'

'Poor old Wayne,' I murmured.

'Yeah,' agreed Howard. 'The police haven't got the manpower to provide twenty-four/seven protection. So they decided to set up safe houses that would take a few people at a time, some of them funding themselves. And this is only the second one in the country. The real aim is to prepare people for their witness protection programme. Goodbye old life, old friends, relatives, job and hello new life, born again like an embryo.'

'So if anything happens here—' I began.

'We'll be shipped out, sweetie,' Howard interrupted, 'but probably kept together.'

I glanced at Fran. She was trembling. 'I'm going to my room,' she said, hurrying away.

Minutes later the trio returned. 'Where are the others?' asked Argon, grim-faced.

'They've gone to their rooms,' answered Howard.

'I want everyone down here now plus internal staff.'

Howard shrugged and went upstairs to pass on the message.

Wayne was the first down, carrying a suitcase, and followed seconds later by a tearful Cheryl. Dave appeared next followed by the chef and a kitchen worker I'd never seen before. Argon didn't need to do a roll call to realize that Fran was missing. He looked straight at me. 'Go and tell her to come down — now!' Gone was any pretence at being our benign counsellor.

Fran wasn't in her room and her wardrobe and drawers were empty. I went slowly downstairs and reluctantly told Argon she had well and truly gone. He snarled, 'The stupid bitch. We'll have to look for her now.' He delegated Dave to go to the right and Rogon to the left. I guessed he viewed them as expendable. 'You others can go to your rooms and stay there until you hear the gong for lunch.'

'I want to leave,' said Wayne.

'Tough shit, mate,' said Argon, leaving his counsellor role well and truly behind. 'No one is going anywhere until we get this sorted. Zoton will escort you to your room. He's armed but he won't kill you. He might break an arm or a leg. You won't even be fit for a walk-on part by the time he's finished with you.'

We all took the hint and went to our rooms. I reasoned that Fran couldn't have got far on foot and she wasn't particularly robust. In fact, gusty Welsh winds could have knocked her over. I slipped a jacket over my arm, picked up my shoulder bag, opened my bedroom door a fraction and, seeing no one, I peered over the balustrade. There was not a soul to be seen so I made my way downstairs and into the kitchen. Inside the kitchen a worker had his back to me and was peeling vegetables. I couldn't see the chef. There was a door marked Fire Exit but I knew that would make a real clang when I left. There was only one thing for it. I moved slowly towards the kitchen worker. He seemed totally engrossed in what he was doing. At least he was until I jabbed two fingers in his back and snarled convincingly, I thought, that a gun was at his back. 'Don't move for ten minutes,' I hissed. He stayed silent; in fact he didn't react at all. I rummaged in my pocket and waved £20 at him.

He smiled. 'Very good,' he said, his accent thick and foreign. 'Very good,' he repeated. As I got to the door I turned. He was already continuing with his vegetables.

I began running towards the farm but was soon out of breath and had to slow to a speedy walk. The sun having shone briefly had now given way to soft drizzle and the temperature had dropped. As I approached the farm by a muddy track with hedges on either side I saw Rogon talking to a man and a woman at the farmhouse door. On her way back there was no way she could avoid seeing me. I turned around and began to run in the opposite direction. Then luckily I found a slight gap in the hedge. I had to force my way through, collecting scratches and nettle stings as I did so. On the other side of the hedge I crouched down hoping she wouldn't see me.

I waited for what seemed a long time until she walked briskly back up the track. I waited until she was out of sight and the farm couple had gone indoors then I made my way to one of several out buildings. In the first there were sheep and newborn lambs; in another were bales of straw and a selection of farm implements. I had a good look round but there was no sign of Fran. There were two more barns. One contained a tractor, the other was empty. I'd almost given up when I noticed in a back field there were dome-shaped huts all over the field and enjoying their freedom were free range pigs. I glanced back nervously towards the farmhouse. I crouched down half expecting a deranged farmer with a shotgun to appear at any minute. There were at least twenty pig huts, one of which Fran might or might not be hiding in. I had to start somewhere.

Although I knew that pigs are clean animals who do not soil where they eat and sleep, outside it was hard to avoid treading in it. I dared not shout out for Fran in case the farmer heard us so I peered into each dark pig-smelling hut, quietly calling out her name. By hut number ten I was beginning to think I was on the wrong track altogether. By number twenty I was sure. My feet were covered in mud, straw and far worse and my patience had evaporated. I was going back. Fran was a grown woman. She'd decided to bolt and that was her choice. Even so I was still worried about her; she'd been in prison for six years and the outside world had changed. I didn't even know if she had any money.

As I was creeping past the farmhouse a dog started barking. I broke into a run but hadn't got far before a male voice boomed out, 'You looking for someone?'

I thought I heard a click as if he were pulling back the safety catch on a shotgun but when I turned around it turned out to be the click of a spade on concrete. As I paused momentarily to answer I saw a face at the farmhouse window. Fran stood there smiling and waving.

CHAPTER TEN

The man with the spade urged me to go in. Inside the farmhouse kitchen a coal fire glowed and the smell of fresh bread emanated from the Aga. Fran seemed delighted to see me. 'Come on in and sit down,' said the woman who I presumed was the farmer's wife. She was stocky with a weather-worn complexion and grey hair in a pony tail.

From the pocket in her apron the handle of a knife protruded but she was smiling.

'I'll leave you two to have a chat,' she said, then added, 'I'm Olwen, by the way.'

She left the kitchen then and I whispered, 'What have you told her?'

Fran sat down beside me. 'I've told her you're my sister and we're trying to escape the clutches of a religious cult.'

'Younger or older sister?'

'Younger.'

'That's all right then,' I said. 'So what now?'

'Olwen says her son will drive us in the Land Rover to the nearest town.'

'Which is?'

'Bala. It seems he has to go there anyway for some reason.'

'And what then, Fran?' I asked. 'Where are you going to go? How will you survive financially?'

'I've got some savings.'

'Have you got a current debit or credit card?'

She shook her head miserably. 'I'll manage.'

'You need help to adjust,' I said, concerned. 'Hubert will help you find the grave of your son but you have to have some sort of plan for afterwards. A place to live, a job . . .'

'Who would employ me with a criminal record?'

I didn't get a chance to answer because Olwen bustled back in. 'You two girls feeling better now you know you're safe?'

'Yes, thank you,' we murmured in unison.

'I hold no truck with the Church of England, see, we're chapel in Wales and proud of it.'

Conversation over lunch was an awkward affair although the thick soup and home-baked bread was delicious. Luckily Fran had mentioned her sister so I was able to fudge my way through the small talk and once we'd got Olwen talking about the farm and the fact that she and her husband hadn't spoken to each other for the last three months it was no surprise that he hadn't joined us.

'He's gone to the pub on his bike. He'll get chips there and a game of darts. He'd rather be in the pub than on the farm. Says he's had enough of it. He wants our Bryn to run it but Bryn has other ideas. He wants to travel but then he's got no money and Hywel won't give him a penny so we're not on speaking terms.'

We offered to wash up and Olwen went off to feed the animals. 'Did Olwen say Bryn was coming for lunch?' I asked.

Fran frowned. 'I'm not sure but I think she said he'd take us *after* lunch.'

'What if he doesn't turn up?'

Fran looked pained. 'I'm not going back. I've waited a long time for my freedom and that place makes me feel claustrophobic.'

'How are you going to escape the media and the death threats?'

'I'll go along with a witness protection plan but not before I'm ready. I'm determined to find my daughter.'

'Why did you agree to stay at Peace Haven in the first place?'

She shrugged. 'My solicitor, Andrew Hanwell, suggested it — in fact he paid for it. He told me it was a luxury halfway house, I'd have more freedom and I'd be safe. In reality I felt safer in the open prison.'

I could only imagine how Fran felt. Not only did she have to adjust to the outside world — although Peace Haven was by no means 'outside' — but it was obvious she struggled to hold her emotions in check. The often taut expression, the chewed fingernails, the tendency to hold her thin body stiffly as if by letting go and relaxing she would fall apart. Would seeing her son's grave for the first time become the catalyst for a major breakdown — and if so would I be to blame? I had no doubt that Hubert would find the information and I also knew that I felt morally obliged to be with her just in case the event proved catastrophic. But was now the right time?

We finished the washing-up and sat at the kitchen table waiting for both Bryn and Olwen, but the minutes ticked by slowly and silently.

'When I was in prison,' said Fran suddenly, 'I wanted to die. For more than a year that was my only ambition. But it's hard to commit suicide; you're watched all the time. I stopped eating but that's not allowed either and I was threatened with force feeding. Then one day I was talking to another prisoner who'd murdered her husband. She didn't have any remorse. "The bastard had it coming to him" she said, but she had a child on the outside in foster care and she loved this child dearly so she behaved well in prison, saved her "wages" to send to her child and focused all her thoughts on her daughter and getting out as soon as possible.'

'Is she still in prison?' I asked.

'No, she died of cancer in hospital but her daughter visited her there and I've been told her death was peaceful in the end.'

At that moment the back door opened and Olwen appeared, taking off her muddy boots and thick socks and leaving them in the porch. In the kitchen she put on her slippers and announced, 'Bryn's not coming. He doesn't want to risk seeing his Da.'

Fran and I exchanged glances. How did she know he wasn't coming? 'Did you phone him?' I asked.

'No, sent him a text.'

I was impressed. 'So you get a mobile phone signal here?'

'Only in the last year, see. Before that we were behind the times. We can't get those digital channels yet. Not that I get time to watch the telly.'

Again Fran and I looked at each other. Decisions had to be made and we were both dithering. Olwen was putting on the kettle again and I could see we'd be drinking tea until it grew dark.

'You've been very kind,' I said, 'but we'll make some phone calls and I'm sure friends will pick us up. We'll go now and leave you in peace.'

'I've got peace in both ears now my Hywel isn't wittering on. You're very welcome to stay.'

'No, we'll go. Thanks so much,' I said.

'That's all right, girls. You'd be much better going to chapel, you know.' Then she added, 'I saw one of those people carriers driving away. I think they've gone. You'll be all right now.'

Olwen waved us goodbye and I had an increasingly sinking feeling that my belongings would be lost forever. Fran noticed that I had no luggage and started apologising.

'We'll go back and have a look round,' I said. 'There might be some way of getting in.'

'You're an optimist,' she said with a faint smile.

It wouldn't be true to say Peace Haven looked *more* deserted. It had looked that way before, and certainly walking around the church and its extension there was no sign of life. The kitchen door was closed and back at the front door, feeling peeved, I gave the ship's bell a good thrashing. Much to my surprise Dave opened the door.

'Where the hell have you two been?' He didn't wait for a reply. 'I've been told,' he said, still sounding annoyed, 'that if you want you can stay here. It's self-catering now — chef's gone and there'll be no more treatments. But if Argon has his way everyone will be back in a few days.'

He ushered us in and told us he'd be staying in the extension and if we wanted him we were to use the phone and dial 6 which would put us straight through to him.

'Cheer up, you two,' he said. 'The bogeyman hasn't got you yet.' He hurried away as if on some mission and we strolled about wondering what to do next. I decided to ring Hubert from the office phone and Fran said she'd check out the kitchen for food.

Thankfully Hubert was in. I explained our predicament and of course he thought the solution was simple. 'I'll collect you tomorrow, no problem.'

'There is a problem,' I said. 'It's Fran.'

I could hear Hubert taking a deep breath. 'I've done a bit of research,' he said. 'From the newspaper accounts she was a cold, heartless killer and I don't think you should be associated with her.'

'That's your opinion, is it? You've never met her . . .'

'Don't have a hissy fit, Kate. I do have some information for you.'

'Oh . . . well, thanks. What is it?'

'Young Benjamin Rowley is buried in Norfolk. St Mary's churchyard just outside Cromer.'

'Norfolk!'

'She'll need a car.'

'She hasn't got one.'

'She must have a friend who has.'

'Yes, me.'

'Kate, I'll collect you tomorrow.'

'You'll be wasting your time. I'm sort of involved now. I feel sorry for her. She's sad and sort of desolate.'

There was a long pause. 'I thought you were sad and desolate,' he said, 'and after a few days away you're back to being your usual stubborn, stroppy self.'

Hubert seemed to be in a hurry to get off the phone and Jasper got scant mention so I felt a little disappointed but I did at least have some news.

I met Fran coming out of the kitchen and we went to sit on sofas in the lounge. Somehow the sound of our voices seemed to echo slightly; so much space and emptiness was unnerving. Fran had organized the ingredients for an evening meal. Apparently we had enough food to cope with a famine in Wales.

'I've got some news,' I said.

She looked at me with a certain eagerness I hadn't seen before.

'Hubert has found out where your son is buried.' Her lower lip trembled slightly. 'He's in St Mary's churchyard just outside Cromer in Norfolk.'

'Thank you,' she murmured.

To say time passed slowly after that would have been a understatement. I tried unsuccessfully to chat about everything from celebrities to politics but Fran had a faraway look in her eyes and simply ignored my comments. So of course I gave up then, picked up a magazine I'd already read and pretended to be engrossed. The silence, lack of music or television hadn't really been a problem for me before but it was now. Much more of this forced inactivity would definitely send me loopy.

After an hour of pretend reading I told Fran I'd start cooking. 'Thank you,' she said dully. In the kitchen she'd left out Arborio rice, mushrooms, bacon, Parmesan cheese and single cream to make a risotto. A glass of wine to drink and add to the risotto seemed like a necessity to me, so I searched the cupboards and huge pantry as if my life depended on it. Then, at the very back of the pantry, I found three bottles with white sticky labels: *Cooking Wine*. They all still had their corks and after rooting through cutlery drawers I managed to find a corkscrew. Of course I then had to taste it to see if it was drinkable. A full glass sampled as I stirred the risotto assured me that it was.

When it was cooked I triumphantly brought in the risotto on a tray and called Fran to the table. 'There's wine as well,' I said.

'I've told you,' she said. 'I don't drink any more.'

'Will it trouble you if I do?'

'No, not at all.' But she didn't sound that convinced so I decided I'd keep nipping back and forth to the kitchen when I wanted wine like a smoker forced to smoke outside.

The risotto tasted fine to me although Fran ate reluctantly and in silence. That fact that I excused myself frequently for a quick slurp couldn't have helped her appetite but the wine tasted good and it had lifted my mood and made me bold.

'Fran,' I said sharply, 'I am willing to drive you to Norfolk and give you any help I can, but you have to communicate with me.'

She didn't even look up.

I tried again but this time I was really blunt. 'Why did you kill your son?'

She looked up sharply. 'I . . . You don't understand.'

'I can't until you tell me.'

'Very well,' she said, sounding resigned. 'I'll tell you. My son was smothered in his cot. You asked why? I have no answer to that. I don't remember doing it. I'd had a lot to drink that night. The police suggested it was drunken rage.'

'And was it?'

'I don't remember being angry.'

'What about evidence?' I queried.

'There was a witness.'

'Who?'

'My daughter, Fiona.'

CHAPTER ELEVEN

'But surely your daughter was only five years old. Did she give evidence?'

Fran swallowed hard. 'Only to a policewoman. She wasn't asked many questions, just, "Where did you see Mummy?", "Where was Benjamin?", "What did Mummy do?", "What did Mummy say?", that sort of thing.'

'How did you both cope?'

Fran flashed me a glance which told me my question was on a par with a reporter asking how a parent felt after losing a child in a dreadful accident.

'I was told by a so-called concerned neighbour in a letter that Fiona stopped speaking after that.'

'And what about you?'

'I was numb with shock. Totally numb. I knew my son was dead and that I must have been responsible so I had to go to prison but everything was unreal for months.'

'Did you get bail?'

'I was kept on remand for several weeks. There were medical and social reports. I saw two psychiatrists, both of whom said I was depressed. My dear husband told them I was obsessively jealous and overly ambitious. I hardly responded to their questions. Benjamin's death had made a large hole in my heart but my brain was also empty. I couldn't think, I couldn't argue. Having done such a dreadful thing I just wanted to die or dissolve — just crumble like dust. I felt I didn't deserve to live.'

'What about Fiona?'

'I felt I might be a risk to her. After all, if I could kill one child then I might kill again.'

'Do you still feel like that?' I asked, horrified.

She shook her head. 'I haven't had a drink since that day and . . .' She broke off as if more words would choke her.

I went to the kitchen to make coffee and we sat in silence for a while. Fran finished her coffee, put down the cup and said, 'Why are you so interested? I'm not a client and I'm not sure I want to rake up the past; it's far too painful.'

Why *was* I so interested? Mystified was the best way to describe my feelings. I simply wanted to understand why a high-flying career woman had cracked under the strain, especially when her actions seemed contrary to her character. My impression, based on what she'd told me, was that she was ambitious, controlled and disciplined, not the sort to go berserk after a couple of gin and tonics. But if I was totally honest with myself, trying to sort out someone else's problems was easier that dwelling on my own.

'Just call it displacement therapy,' I said eventually. 'Perhaps I'm just a person who *needs* to know.'

Fran gave a slight nod. 'I know what you mean. When I was working I tried to get to know my clients, firstly trying to find out where their marriages had gone wrong and then finding the best solution for their situation. I couldn't repair their partnerships but I listened and made suggestions. Sometimes they left my office having communicated for the first time in months. Just occasionally they managed to remain friends.'

I wasn't sure that Fran was any more willing to open up but I felt that, in time, a thaw was a strong possibility. She started to clear the table and as we washed up in the kitchen she told me she planned to go to bed as she felt very tired. We'd just finished tidying up when Dave appeared.

'How's it going, ladies?' he asked. He didn't wait for a reply but added, 'Argon's been in touch; he's sending a car for Fran early tomorrow morning at five a.m. You're free to do what you want, Kate. You'll have a claim for the return of your fees.'

'What if I don't want to go?' asked Fran, looking worried.

'Might be best, love,' he said. 'That car you saw contained a couple of local reporters out to make a name for themselves. A bit of loose talk from the hairdresser, it's thought. Best to make a run for it before they sell the story to the local papers.'

As he walked away he said cheerily, 'Things could be worse, girls; they could have been from the *News of the World*.'

'What was that supposed to mean?' I asked.

Fran sighed. 'The *News of the World* was particularly vitriolic about me. You know the sort of thing: *Rich bitch kills own child*. Followed by *Top lawyer's neglect of husband and family*. For that I have to thank my ex-husband. He sold his story for several thousand pounds. I'm sure the readers loved it.' She gave a wry smile. 'You see, I was fairly well known for getting larger than average settlements for my clients. Obviously that rattled the media and soon all the tabloids were after anyone who'd ever said good morning to me. And I mean that literally: my neighbours, the local delicatessen, even a wine bar near my office. That proved rich pickings. According to the newspapers I was in at lunch times and evenings not just once a week, but every day. Everything they said about my life was a distortion of the truth.'

I really didn't know what to say. I read newspapers, of course, and sometimes the less respectable tabloids that relied more on gossip and sensationalism than news and facts, but they passed a harmless ten minutes and I could complete the crossword. The lies and half-truths that I sometimes found interesting and titillating never really caused me to think about the damage they did to individuals and families. Whatever had caused Fran to commit murder, she'd served a prison sentence, lost her husband, sister and friends, and she suffered every day. Surely that was punishment enough.

Back in the lounge I asked Fran what exactly she wanted to do. She sat on the sofa, held her hands to her face and rocked herself.

'I can tell Dave to stop the driver coming,' I said. 'Come back to Longborough with me and I'll drive you to Norfolk and then we can take it from there.'

'Why would you want to put yourself out for me?' she muttered, still rocking herself gently.

'You need a friend, I need a mission.'

'You make it sound simple, Kate.'

'It is simple. You have to move on. If that means reinventing yourself then that's what you need to do. New appearance, new name, new life.'

'But I'd be living a lie.'

'True, but you might be happier.'

'I don't expect happiness. Just peace of mind would help . . .' She broke off. 'I thought that after all this time I would be able to remember what happened that night.'

'It could have been that your actions were so . . . tragic that your mind tried to protect you from the full horror.'

She shrugged and continued to rock back and forth. 'Why can't I cry? I want to. I'm crying inside.'

It took her half an hour to make a decision and then I made my first trip to the new extension to find Dave. The door was open. I didn't knock. I crept into what was a combined kitchen and lounge. There was no smell of cooking and everything was tidy and anonymous. Off the kitchen was another door, slightly ajar. I padded quietly to the doorway. Dave was lounging back in a swivel chair reading a newspaper. In front of him were several CCTV monitors showing every room. The black and white images were motionless except for Fran who now sat upright and still. She looked vulnerable and desperately alone — or at least she should have been alone but was being spied on by Dave, who I suspected was a retired cop.

Without looking up he said, 'I know you're there, Kate. What do you want?'

I walked into the surveillance room. 'Call off the driver, will you? Fran wants to go her own way.'

'Silly girl,' he said. 'She's had some nasty threats and this world is full of nutters. He'll find her.'

'Thanks for being so reassuring.'

'Howard's copped it already,' said Dave as casually as if he was telling me it was raining.

'What do you mean? What's happened?'

'He's been shot, but don't worry, love, he'll make it.'

'I don't believe you.'

'That's up to you. Howard's cover had been blown and the drug ring he was involved with had put a price on his head.'

'Where is he now?'

'I can't tell you that now, can I?'

I was shocked. If he had protection how could he have been found so soon? When I asked Dave that very question, he shrugged.

'Drug money buys surveillance equipment, high-powered rifles and loose tongues.'

'I won't be telling Fran,' I said, 'and I'd prefer it if you didn't either.'

'Right you are, love. It's your call but she should know her life is at risk. One joker is putting threats out on the internet.'

'But they can be traced, can't they?'

'Not quickly, and if internet cafes are being used, maybe never.'

Subdued, I returned to Fran. She too looked worried and anxious. 'I'm going to bed,' she said. Then she tried to smile. 'Big day tomorrow. Will your Hubert be . . .' She broke off.

'He's very kind,' I said. 'He'll want to suss you out but he's very understanding.' I didn't add that he was also very protective of me.

I didn't sleep well that night. The utter silence bordered on sensory deprivation and my mind was in overdrive.

About three a.m. I finally fell asleep only to be woken by the sound of a door closing. Ignore it, was my first thought but I couldn't and groggily I grabbed my dressing gown and peered out of my bedroom door. Fran was walking downstairs barefoot and in her pyjamas. I waited, wondering where she was going. She disappeared into the lounge area and seconds later she reappeared carrying a magazine. I closed my door. I was getting suspicious and tiredness was making me paranoid because it crossed my mind that if she could smother her child in the night then she could also smother me.

CHAPTER TWELVE

Hubert arrived late morning and although he was civil to Fran I could tell he disapproved of my bringing her back with me. Traffic on the journey was light and Fran fell asleep within minutes but it took me half an hour. Long enough to promise Hubert I'd be careful, because although he could see my mood had improved he was worried I'd face a setback if things went pear-shaped. I didn't want to talk about Fran or Stalag Peace Haven in case she was feigning sleep.

Back at Humberstone's Jasper greeted me with circles, twirls and jumping as high as he could. I sat down to cuddle him but as soon as he saw Fran he leapt from my lap and did the same routine for her. Most strangers encounter a bit of yapping and suspicious sniffing, and if they past muster he starts to tail wag and jump up. Fran, in contrast, had been instantly accepted. Jasper sat on her lap and she stroked him gently as he licked her free hand. Hubert was unable to hide his astonishment and I think she went up a decimal point in his estimation.

After lunch Fran asked if she could go to the guest room. Hubert raised his eyebrows and was even more surprised when Jasper toddled behind her without a backward glance at us.

'Perhaps she smells right,' he said.

I think we both felt a somewhat discarded. What did she have to offer that we didn't? 'Jasper might be annoyed with me for going away,' I suggested.

Hubert frowned. 'Could be he feels sorry for her, senses she's unhappy.'

We didn't come to any conclusions and Hubert soon made it obvious he wanted to talk.

'I've done some research,' he said with a hint of pride. 'There's a pile of newspapers in your office all relating to the Rowley case.'

'How did you get those?'

'Friend of a client knew an old man who collects newspapers like some people collect stamps — eccentric of course, but there's a great selection for you to read.'

I could hardly wait to get into my office and read them but Hubert had other ideas.

'What do you make of her?' he asked.

I thought for a moment. 'A sad, lonely, unhappy, nervous woman but not volatile or dangerous in any way.'

'Not a hard ambitious drunk then?'

'I think she *was* ambitious,' I said, 'and she admitted that she did have a few drinks after work but she doesn't seem hard or unfeeling. Jasper obviously doesn't think so either.'

'Pity Jasper wasn't the judge,' said Hubert with a wry smile.

'Killing her son,' I said firmly, 'seems to me to be totally out of character. To be a divorce lawyer I would think needs patience and perseverance.'

'And being a wife and mother,' added Hubert. 'Go on, go and read the reports and then we'll decide what to do.'

'*I'll* decide what to do,' I muttered as I walked away. Hubert had for some time grown tired of the funeral business. I knew he wanted us to be an investigation team on a more professional footing but I was a little afraid he'd take over completely or prove to be better at it than me. I knew he would argue that PIs didn't work alone these days, which was true, but I wasn't overly ambitious. To earn a modest living and try to solve problems was enough for me.

In my office Hubert had placed a huge stack of newspapers. It was a pity he hadn't summarized them for me. He had stacked them in order though and left me a little note: *Keep tidy. Do not damage*. I sat down and began at the start — the reports of Benjamin's death. The initial reports were in most papers of the *Tragic Baby Death of Top Lawyer* variety. The cause of death was given as uncertain and foul play had not been ruled out. The next day, a woman believed to be the baby's mother was helping with enquiries.

The low-key approach didn't last long and once Francesca Rowley had been formally charged with murder the downmarket tabloids began converging on the Rowley house and interviews started to appear. Husband, nanny, cleaner, sister and even the next-door neighbour were all asked to express their thoughts and opinions. The consensus at that point seemed to be that Fran was a loving mother, reserved and very hard-working but had looked tired and drawn in the weeks before Benjamin died. Asked if they believed Fran could be capable of suffocating her son the answer seemed to be an unequivocal no.

Reports of the initial hearing caused headline news when Fran entered her plea of guilty. She was reported to be calm, in control and showing no remorse. Hard-faced, cold and ambitious was a description from one newspaper. I had planned to take notes but a knock at my door and Hubert's immediate entry made an unwelcome interruption.

'She's in the kitchen, Kate. I don't know what to say to her. You'll have to come.'

I followed him to the kitchen where Fran sat staring into space. She didn't make any movement or sign that she knew we were present. Hubert raised his eyebrows and then I noticed that Jasper sat at, or rather on, her foot. I lifted up his reluctant little body and handed him to Hubert suggesting that Jasper needed a walk. Hubert seemed relieved and left the kitchen with Jasper still in his arms.

I touched her arm and she gazed up at me miserably. 'We need to talk, Fran. If you want me to take you to Norfolk I need to know you're going to be able to cope.'

'I've coped so far, haven't I?'

I didn't answer that. 'I've been reading the newspapers about your case.'

'Why?'

'I investigate; it's almost second nature to me.'

She sighed deeply. 'I pleaded guilty because I must have killed my son. There was no one else in the house. The police convinced me that I had to be responsible. My lack of memory didn't mitigate my crime.'

'Were you drunk?'

'I remember having two gin and tonics but I was questioned about the measure. I guess I could have had two doubles or even triples. I remember that my last drink emptied the bottle.'

'Did you stagger upstairs or were you walking normally?'

Fran looked at me in despair. 'Does it make any difference? It happened and I killed my beautiful boy.' She stood up as if to go.

'Doesn't it trouble you,' I said, 'that you behaved totally out of character?'

'Of course it troubles me,' she snapped. 'There hasn't been a day since that night that I haven't been troubled. What do you think I am — a monster?'

'No, of course not. But I want you to take me through the events of that evening.'

She sighed. 'Don't you think I've gone over it a thousand times?'

'This is the first time for me, so indulge me.'

She shrugged in capitulation and sat down. 'I arrived home about eight p.m.'

'Did you drive?'

'Yes.'

'Tell me exactly what you did from the minute you arrived home.'

'I came in through the front door. Erin, the nanny, was ready to go out. She said both children were asleep and she'd just checked them.'

'You had complete trust in her?'

'I wouldn't have employed her if I didn't trust her. She was devoted to the children.'

'Did you check on the children?'

'No. I trusted Erin. I walked into the sitting room and took off my jacket, kicked off my shoes and poured myself a gin and tonic.'

'A large one?'

'Yes, a large one — at least a double. Then I sprawled on the sofa.'

'What about your evening meal?'

'I'd had lunch that day. A few of us from the office had gone to the wine bar round the corner from the office.'

'What time was that?'

'What difference does it make?' she asked irritably.

'You're doing fine, Fran, just keep going. My questions might seem banal but they may help you remember small things that may be important.'

'We left the office promptly at one p.m.'

'And what did you eat for lunch?'

She raised her eyebrows at that. 'If you must know I had a prawn salad.'

'So from just after one p.m. you had nothing more to eat?'

'No. I was too tired to cook.'

'So your gin and tonic had an immediate effect?'

'Yes. I drank that, poured another, and then I fell asleep.'

'What time did you wake up?'

'I'm not sure — after ten. I was feeling groggy and I went upstairs . . .' She broke off. 'I went to the bathroom first. I felt so dopey I washed my face . . .' She broke off again, frowning.

'What's the matter?' I asked.

'I've just remembered something about the bathroom.'

'What about it?'

'The toilet seat was up. I used the en-suite bathroom and Neil always put the seat down because I complained if he didn't.'

'Anything else?'

She shook her head but with no conviction.

'There is something else,' I said. 'Close your eyes and think of yourself in the bathroom. You've just washed your face.'

Eyes closed she sat for several seconds then she said, 'There was a smell of flowers but I don't know what type.' She opened her eyes and smiled. 'Strange I've not remembered that before.'

'That's because it didn't seem important but maybe it is.' We were on a roll and I didn't want to give up now. 'Close your eyes again,' I said. 'You're leaving the bathroom and your bedroom — where did you go next?'

There was a long pause. 'I'm going into Ben's room. I walk towards his cot. I see the pillow. I lift the pillow and throw it away. He was so white. I touched his cheek. It was cold. I knew he was dead.'

'Did you pick him up?'

'Yes.'

'Did you try to resuscitate him?'

'No. He was dead. He was so cold.'

'Where is Fiona?'

'She was there, standing by the door . . .' Her voice began to break. 'I think she ran away.'

'What were you doing then?'

'I . . . I was rocking him backwards and forwards,' she whispered. Silent tears trickled down her face as she opened her eyes. She stood up and walked out of the kitchen. I wanted to go after her but I decided she needed to be alone. Had I gone too far? Was it fair to her? I was more than relieved when Hubert returned.

'What's upset you?' he asked.

I looked at Hubert's troubled face and realized he knew me better than my own mother. It was a sobering thought. 'Fran's been telling me about the night her son died.'

'He didn't just die, he was murdered,' said Hubert as he filled the kettle. 'I don't think you're handling her very well. She isn't a client. You're doing her a favour but that's all. She wants to forget, not have the past raked over.'

'She wants to find her daughter, Fiona. I could help her.'

His facial expression showed either disapproval or disbelief.

'Where's Jasper?' I asked, trying to fend off any further criticism.

'He's followed her. Don't try to change the subject. Look at the facts. The woman has admitted murdering her son. She's served a prison sentence, she's out now and she's got to find her own salvation.'

I fell silent as Hubert made a pot of tea and I sat and stared out of the kitchen window. After a while Hubert asked, 'Are you sulking?'

'I am not! I'm thinking.'

'Leave this one, Kate. Let her be. She's surely got friends and relatives who can help her.'

'That's the point,' I said. 'Her friends deserted her, even her sister. Her only visitor during her time in prison was a solicitor colleague.'

It was Hubert's turn to fall silent. We drank tea and I succumbed to the lure of chocolate biscuits.

'What if,' I began cautiously, 'what if Fran did *not* kill her son?'

Hubert nearly choked on his biscuit. 'She pleaded guilty. The police found no evidence of a forced entry.'

'It seems strange that she said that Benjamin was very cold.'

'So?'

'Time of death was placed sometime between eight p.m. when the nanny left and about ten p.m. Fran arrived home at eight p.m. She says she drank two gin and tonics and then fell asleep. It was Friday night, she was probably exhausted after working all week—'

'She could be lying,' interrupted Hubert. 'Once the nanny had left she could have gone upstairs and killed her son before having a drink.'

'Point taken, but she pleaded guilty so why lie?'

Hubert shrugged. 'Perhaps she thought she'd get a lighter sentence if she was drunk.'

'There is no evidence that she was drunk. No blood tests were taken at the time and when the police came to the conclusion that she was guilty it was too late.'

'So she didn't admit her guilt straight away?'

'I'm not sure. I think the police convinced her that only she could have been responsible and in grief and shock she went along with that idea.'

'You're just guessing. Where's the evidence?'

'Precisely,' I said. 'The police didn't have any real evidence against her. They *needed* a confession.'

'Whatever,' said Hubert with a slightly dismissive shrug. 'She pleaded guilty.'

'There was an eye witness.'

'Who?' he asked sharply.

'Her daughter, Fiona. She walked into the room just as Fran lifted the pillow.'

'She was only five years old.' I stared at Hubert until his brain neurones kicked into gear. 'You're not suggesting . . .' he began.

'I am suggesting just that. It doesn't take much strength to suffocate a small child.'

Hubert sipped his tea thoughtfully. 'You think that's why Fran pleaded guilty?'

'It's one theory anyway. I do have others,' I said, thinking of the raised lavatory seat and the smell of flowers.

'Leave it alone, Kate. If your half-baked theory is true then Fran made the ultimate sacrifice and she won't thank you if you suggest her daughter could have killed her own brother.'

I sighed inwardly. Hubert could be right. Should I just let things be? Is the truth really important at any cost?

Later, alone in my room, I sat on the bed reading articles that followed the trial. Some were sympathetic to the stress of the *have it all woman*, others less so. Sympathy lay with single mothers who had to work but mothers who had a husband and lived in Holland Park and still chose to work were thought to be selfish and self-seeking. Fran's apparent lack of remorse and tears, her 'cold reserve' led one journalist to suggest it showed a lack of maternal feeling. *Was she a woman who should never have had children*? There was very little criticism of Neil Rowley; in fact his media attention was entirely positive. He was reported to be a 'hands-on' father who had chosen to work from home to enable him to further his wife's career. I thought this was bullshit but the bias was blatant and constant. Fran Rowley had been condemned as an unnatural mother and some newspapers had even criticized the judge for his light sentence.

I read until my eyes felt heavy then I tidied away the newspapers, took a quick bath and was in bed by ten thirty. Jasper scrabbling at my door woke me. It was two thirty a.m. I thought it was unlike Jasper to wake in the night and as I opened the door to let him in I noticed the guest room door was slightly ajar and the light was on. I padded barefoot towards her door. I called Fran's name softly and quietly swung the door open. I called out again. There was no reply. I searched the bathroom, the kitchen, the lounge. Then I roused Hubert to tell him that Fran had gone.

CHAPTER THIRTEEN

Hubert, disgruntled at being woken, muttered, 'I knew that woman would be trouble. What do you want me to do? Have you looked downstairs?'

I had not. Downstairs housed the office, reception, the catering suite, the chapel of rest and the cold room. It was eerie in the dark and not somewhere I'd choose to explore on my own. As Hubert slipped on his plaid dressing gown over his plaid pyjamas Jasper appeared and was obviously keen to join our 'game' of finding Fran. In fact he led the way and forced the pace. Hubert switched on all the lights as we went and Jasper sniffed around, excitedly wagging his tail. There was no sign of life in the house of death and we were both mystified. Humberstone's was fitted with burglar alarms and fairly recently a CCTV camera at the front and back doors. If she hadn't left the building, where was she? I looked upwards thinking she might have gone up to the roof. Hubert's face dropped but then an excited yap from Jasper led us to the basement stairs. The coffins were kept in the basement. We hurriedly followed Jasper.

Even with the lights on the basement was dim and shadowy. The coffins were arranged in tiers; the small coffins for babies and children were slipped under the first tier. Fran sat on the floor by an open-lidded tiny white coffin. She looked gaunt and white-faced but she did respond to Jasper when he sat by her side by abstractedly stroking his head. She looked up sharply and stared at me. 'I didn't do it. I know now I didn't do it.'

'You mean you didn't kill Benjamin?'

She nodded.

'After all this time,' I said as I sat down beside her, 'what's changed your mind?'

'I couldn't sleep so I wandered about . . .' She paused. 'That's not quite true. I did have a purpose. I wanted to see a child's coffin. I wasn't allowed to say goodbye to my son. I thought seeing a coffin would help me imagine it. I could see him at peace . . .' Her voice became a near whisper. 'I opened the lid and it was like lifting the pillow and I knew then as sure . . . as sure as night follows day that I could *not* have covered my child's face even if I'd been very drunk. I couldn't even close an empty coffin.'

I put my arm around her and Hubert signalled that he was leaving. 'Don't go,' she said. 'I want to ask you something.'

'Fire away,' said Hubert, looking uncomfortable.

'The coffin is very plain,' she said. 'Are they all the same?'

'No,' he said in his softest voice. 'The family can choose the lining but usually it's padded white silk with a tiny pillow. The child holds a posy or a favourite toy.' Then he added gently, 'I'm sure your husband gave him the very best funeral.'

'Thank you,' she murmured.

Hubert picked up Jasper and returned upstairs. We continued to sit on the floor. My backside was cold and one foot had developed pins and needles but Fran didn't want to move.

'I know what you're thinking,' she said. 'You thought that perhaps I was protecting Fiona, but she loved her baby brother. In her own little way she was motherly and protective towards him. Only a very disturbed child commits murder. Fifi was a happy, normal child. She loved Ben like another little mother. She had one loving grandmother back then and she adored her father. Afterwards . . .' Her voice cracked with emotion. 'Afterwards she didn't speak for three days. We were both in shock.'

My discomfort at sitting on the stone floor was such that I had to stand up. I eased myself up less nimbly than a fit eighty-year-old and then helped Fran up. She stared at the coffin for several seconds whilst I stretched and stamped my feet to ease my pins and needles.

'I can't close the coffin lid,' she said. So we left that tiny coffin lying there and walked upstairs to the kitchen.

Hubert had made tea and arranged chocolate biscuits rather decoratively on a plate.

We drank and ate the biscuits in silence for a while then Fran said, 'You will help me, won't you, Kate?'

'What do you want me to do?'

She stared at me. 'I want you to find out who murdered my son.'

Hubert took a sharp intake of breath. 'I don't think Kate can take that on,' he said. 'You pleaded guilty after all.'

'I'll decide what I'm going to do,' I said frostily. Hubert bit down hard on a chocolate biscuit. His reaction meant I was obviously going to do my very best. After all, it was a challenge now that he'd had thrown down the gauntlet.

'I pleaded guilty,' said Fran, in a firm voice, 'because the police persuaded me that I'd wiped it from my memory, that no one else could have done it. They told me I was angry and jealous and the gin just tipped me over the edge. They put it to me that Ben's crying irritated me. I couldn't deny that it did sometimes but most of the time Ben was such a happy, easy-going baby. Ask anyone — ask Erin . . .' She broke off. 'I'm sure now I didn't do it.'

The silence in the room was broken by Hubert. 'I think we should all go back to bed.' Then he added, 'While you're both in Norfolk I'll do some sleuthing on the internet. Which agency did you get your nanny from?'

Fran looked taken aback and I was getting increasingly irritated with Hubert trying to take charge. 'The Mayflower, I think; they supplied our cleaner too. Why?'

Before Hubert could speak I said, 'Because Erin may know where your husband is.'

Fran shrugged. 'I doubt it. He doesn't want to be found so he wouldn't tell her just in case she told me, although I don't think that she would.'

'She didn't contact you . . . ever?'

Fran shook her head. 'She adored Ben; after all, she'd helped look after him since the day he was born, so after that night she made it clear that she and God would never ever forgive me.'

I sensed that Hubert wanted to butt in but I flashed him a glance he couldn't misinterpret and he stayed silent.

Fran went back to bed then. She looked exhausted but I thought she carried herself differently, more confidently, as though guilt had literally been lifted from her shoulders.

Hubert began rinsing cups with his back towards me. I sensed he was miffed and after a few moments he turned and said, 'I know I'm not the world's leading expert on murder, even though I'm pretty good on death itself. But if it was an outsider who killed the baby then what the hell was the motive?'

That question stopped me in my tracks. 'OK,' I said, 'you're right. I do need help. We need to know far more about Fran, because her change of mind might be an aberration. She could still have done it.'

'Using long words won't solve it,' said Hubert with a smile tinged with triumph. 'You're concentrating on Fran, but supposing she wasn't the target.'

'You mean the motive for Benjamin's murder was a grudge against her husband?'

'Or the nanny.'

I had to admit that thought hadn't occurred to me but since Fran had maintained that she was guilty there had been no reason to suspect anyone else. As I left Hubert sitting in the kitchen reading yesterday's newspaper I patted his large bald spot. 'Go to it,' I said. 'I'll be expecting great things of you.'

'You cheeky madam,' he said. 'Sometimes I feel really unappreciated.'

In my room I felt wide awake so I made a list. Not of suspects but of the friends and colleagues of Fran and Neil. I know little about divorce law, never having been married, but I'd read enough to know that marriage break-ups could lead to misery, poverty, stress, illness — and, worse still, suicide and murder. There was a possibility that one of Fran's clients, outraged, perhaps demented at a settlement, could have planned a horrific revenge.

Neil, once a chartered accountant, could have upset a client or more likely an irate husband or lover. The nanny probably had a boyfriend or boyfriends who could have come looking for her in a jealous rage. Being devoted to Benjamin she'd undoubtedly talked about him. A possessive, insecure young man creeping up to the room she sometimes shared with Ben might have been overcome with rage at the sight of him.

No scenario was completely convincing and there were so many possibilities that my head began to buzz. Two major questions remained. How did the murderer gain access to the house? And, far more importantly, why?

* * *

The drive to Norfolk was long and tedious, punctuated by both rain and hail. The sky was grey and bleak and although I wanted to talk Fran slept for long stretches.

We stopped for lunch at a village pub, the traditional type, complete with horse brasses but serving meals at an untraditionally inflated price. It was worth it, however, for the glowing coal fire, the cheerful staff and Fran's reaction. As we settled down with a pot of coffee and began reading the menu she said, 'This is really lovely.' Then in a whisper she added, 'When I was in prison I'd long to be in a country pub by a river on a summer's day. This is more like winter but it's still a real treat.'

She chose plain salmon with salad. I chose steak and kidney pie. 'A salad in prison is a rarity,' she explained. 'Even then two soggy lettuce leaves, half a tomato and two slices of cucumber is the best you can hope for and salmon certainly never appeared on the menu.'

While we waited for our meals I asked Fran about her work as a divorce lawyer.

'It's seems so long ago,' she said thoughtfully. 'But I do remember always feeling under tremendous pressure. Clients' emotions were so raw and sometimes you saw your own problems reflected back at you.'

'Was there anyone who could have held a grudge against you?'

She managed a wry smile. 'Oh, yes. Several. Mostly men who felt their wives had got the best deal. Or they felt short-changed about access to their children.'

'Can you remember any names?'

'I do remember one. A really nasty, violent thug. I have to admit even I was scared of him. He was a professional footballer, could still be, I suppose. Kieran Leyland.'

I'd seen some coverage of his violence on TV. He was a good footballer but always on a short fuse. It was also suggested he was a heavy drinker. The last I'd heard of him he was playing for a non-league side, his glory days being over.

'Did he ever threaten you?' I asked.

'He did but I got a little hardened to threats.'

'What did he say?'

'He came rampaging into the office one day saying I was a lying, devious bitch who had poisoned his wife's mind against him. "If it's poison you want, you fucking bitch, I can afford the best." Those were his exact words. I didn't know what he meant but it wasn't exactly a death threat as such.'

'As near as damn it, I'd say.'

'The threats I had in prison were much more detailed. I was going to be crippled for life, my children would disappear, my house would burn down, et cetera, et cetera.'

I gazed at her. Her voice and demeanour were calm and matter-of-fact, as if death threats were relatively normal.

'No wonder the police suggested Peace Haven.'

'To be honest, I don't think the police could have cared less where I went or what happened to me. My colleague and only surviving friend Malcolm suggested it.'

'He really has been a good friend to you, hasn't he?'

'I couldn't have survived without him. His visits really lifted my spirits and he always found time to write to me.'

'Are you in love with him?'

She shook her head. 'No, but I love him like a brother. He's married anyway.'

Our meal arrived then and Fran ate her salad with real enjoyment, whilst I counted calories, managing not to let one single calorie escape as if by counting them they mattered less.

'Have you been in touch with Malcolm since your release?' I asked over our final coffee.

'No. His wife knew he was visiting me but now I'm free I might upset her. She might think I'm being demanding. He works very long hours and I know he's planning to find me a rural retreat to rent.'

'Perhaps you'd better phone him tonight.'

'I'll do that.'

We left the pub and continued our journey, glimpsing the occasional sliver of sunshine which, together with a full stomach, raised our spirits. At least for a while until Norfolk began to seem endless with its flat landscape and the day crept towards evening. I blamed myself for our late start but after our disturbed night we'd slept late and now I had to find somewhere to stay before dark.

Eventually just outside a small village I saw a sign with an arrow pointing down a lane: the Black Kettle Guest House. I found it half a mile down the lane. The garish Black Kettle sign swung from a gibbet-style frame. The front door was black and the windows were framed in black. Two hanging baskets either side of the front door contained dying winter pansies. I turned to Fran, 'What do you think?' I asked.

'It's one better than a deconsecrated church.'

I wasn't so sure. I was about to ring the doorbell when Fran touched my arm.

'There's something I have to tell you,' she said anxiously. I was pretty sure it was something to do with not having any money so with a finger poised over the doorbell I said, 'Tell me later.'

'No, I have to tell you now,' she answered as the doorbell chimed like a wartime siren.

CHAPTER FOURTEEN

Fran was silenced by the eerie chimes and by an elderly man with wispy white hair, wearing a grey cardigan and baggy grey trousers, who answered the door and viewed us suspiciously. 'Have you booked, miss?' he asked. 'We don't take casuals.'

'No,' I said, 'we just need somewhere to stay for the night.'

He looked us both up and down slowly. 'I'm sure you'll find a place in the village.'

'It's bucketing with rain,' I said. 'And we've never been to Norfolk before. It's just the one night.'

He slipped on the spectacles that hung from a gold chain around his neck and stared at us again. 'We run a wartime experience here,' he said. 'We're just about to put up the blackout curtains. We've got a double room. Its fifty pounds each, breakfast and one supper included. The door is locked at eleven p.m.'

I looked at Fran and although we were standing in a covered porch the rain was whipping around our ankles. She nodded.

'Come on in then,' he said. 'I'm Mr Martin and I run this place with my friend Mr Silas. And you are?'

'Kate Kinsella and Fran Benson.' Benson was my mother's maiden name and I thought it safer than Rowley because keeping her own name seemed odd and risky in the circumstances.

'Follow me, ladies. Supper is at seven on the dot so you've just got time to unpack.'

Our shoes sounded loud on the bare lino and although the stairs were carpeted in a dull brown the carpet itself was worn and shiny and the floorboards creaked. Our room had a ghastly flower print on the walls, a single dark oak wardrobe and a double bed with a rose pink eiderdown. Mr Martin deftly pulled down a black blind and closed the black curtains. 'We're expecting an air raid tonight. When you hear it you must make your way quickly to the cellar.'

When he'd left the room we stood open-mouthed and then burst out laughing, collapsing on the bed as we did so. When Fran finally stopped her cheeks were flushed pink.

'That's the best laugh I've had,' she said breathlessly, 'since a middle-aged bitch of a PO slipped on a potato skin and showed her thong.'

Like all belly laughs or good sex, once it's over it feels like a bit of an anti-climax. I waited for Fran to tell me what was so urgent outside but she had begun unpacking and was arranging her pyjamas very neatly on the bed.

'This might be the most eccentric B&B in the country,' I said, trying to break the uneasy silence that had no fallen, 'but at least we do have a hospitality tray of sorts.' I'd only just noticed the tin tray that contained cups and saucers, a tea pot, loose tea, a tea strainer plus a tin of condensed milk and a bottle of Camp coffee. Under a piece of grease-proof paper were two slices of Battenberg cake with that line of garish pink running through it.

I glanced at the old-fashioned alarm clock on the bedside table. It was very nearly six thirty. 'Let's hope,' I said, 'that the food at least is from the twenty-first century.'

Our fellow guests, all in uniform, were already seated in the dining room at the communal table that was covered with a maroon oilcloth and decorated with a vase of drooping daffodils in the middle surrounded by bottles of brown and tomato sauces. Mr Martin introduced us as Miss Kinsella and Miss Benson from the land army. There were four other couples, introduced as Able Seaman Jack Jones and ARP Warden Mrs Elizabeth Jones; Pilot Officer Frank Board and WAAF Sister Avril Board; Sergeant Bill Blenkinsopp and his wife, QA Nurse Lillian, and Private Raymond Cross and Wren Mrs Jennifer Cross.

Fran and I both wore jeans and jumpers so we looked fairly rural. We tried to keep a straight face and it would have been easier if the guests had been pensioners but the oldest person there was only forty or so. Mr Martin requested silence for grace. 'Thank you for what we are about to receive, and may God and Winston Churchill protect us from the wicked Hun.'

What we did receive was a passable vegetable soup with bread and marge followed by rissoles with fried potatoes and cabbage washed down with home-made wine of unknown origin. Whilst we ate we listened to speeches by Winston Churchill and the propaganda of Lord Haw Haw. Our dessert was bread and butter pudding and another variety of home-made wine, which tasted vile but, judging by the resulting laughter and general bonhomie, was high in alcohol content. It seemed we were back in 1942, and the other guests were very well informed on the war's progress so our contribution to the conversation was extremely limited. The evening had been surreal and after some milky Camp coffee we were all singing old wartime songs until eleven p.m. when Mr Martin told us it was time for bed and reminded us that when the sirens sounded we were to make our way to the cellar.

We hadn't made any friends but it was interesting to hear of the imaginary derring-do of the male guests and watch the couples acting as if their forty-eight-hour passes were real as they held hands and gazed into each other's eyes with real intensity and longing.

Back in our room I wondered if the guests should get a life or if this was perhaps the next new trend for the hotel trade? After all, murder mystery weekends had been popular for years. I decided that if I ever gave up the agency I'd like to run a themed B&B, although quite what theme I'd choose foxed me. Fran had clearly enjoyed herself and it was only now I realized she'd drunk a few glasses of the home-made wine. She'd gone immediately to the bathroom and I could hear her vomiting. I guessed it had been self-induced. When she reappeared she looked pale and downcast. 'I was stupid to drink that stuff. I thought the alcohol content would be lower than normal wine. I've let myself down again.'

'Don't beat yourself up,' I said. 'You can't change human frailty.'

'I just get more stupid as I get older,' she muttered as she climbed into bed. I felt shattered and minutes later I too climbed into bed and was asleep within minutes.

* * *

It seemed only minutes later that the siren sounded. I stared at my bedside clock. It was one a.m. and I was in a mad, mad world. 'I'm not going down to the cellar,' I muttered from under the bedclothes. There was no answer from Fran. The siren continued and then there came the droning noise of aircraft overhead.

Footsteps thumped downstairs and then back upstairs and soon someone was banging on our door shouting, 'It's a raid. Come on, get up!' This was followed by the sound of blasts and explosions. Wearily we left our beds, slipped on our dressing gowns and made our way downstairs to the cellar.

Our fellow guests sat huddled on cushions against the cellar walls under the shadowy light of a dim bulb hanging from the ceiling. Mr Martin was busy handing round mugs of cocoa but of Mr Silas there was still no sign. He was obviously only the cook and therefore above participating in mock air raids. The explosive sounds were less harsh in the cellar but some enthusiastic time-warper decided, in an effort to raise morale, to start a sing-song.

Fran cast me a weary glance and rested her head on my shoulder. 'I've done something I'm ashamed of,' she whispered in my ear.

'Haven't we all,' I wanted to say but I was pretty sure that the middle of an air raid, even a mock one, wasn't the right time to unburden anyone's conscience. There was a particularly loud bang at that moment and Fran whispered something but I didn't hear a word. She repeated it as silence fell so that her soft voice seemed to echo and bounce around the walls.

'I think I'm pregnant.'

CHAPTER FIFTEEN

My mouth literally dropped open. 'How the hell did you manage that?' I blurted out.

There was silence all around until someone sniggered and Mr Martin said loudly, 'Come on then, let's have a rousing chorus of "We'll meet again" before the all clear sounds.'

Fran and I sang like automatons and when the all clear did sound I bundled her quickly up the cellar steps before any of the others could offer either their congratulations or condolences.

In our room Fran sat on the bed staring ahead. I now felt like an irate mother whose protected and supervised daughter announces she is in trouble.

How? When? Why? These were questions I needed answering but I stayed silent and gritted my teeth.

Eventually Fran looked up. 'It was a couple of months ago. The prison arranges release-preparation days. I was allocated a male probation officer. We went to Brighton and I suppose the sun, the sea and good food went to my head. We . . .' She hesitated. 'We had sex in the back of his car.'

I was more than exasperated. 'For an intelligent woman you can be a bloody stupid bitch,' I snapped.

Her reply was swift and angry. 'Have you ever been without a man's arms around you for more than six years? Have you ever longed to see more than a patch of sky or watch the tide come in or see trees and grass and children running free . . .' She broke off. 'I was weak and he was young and attractive.'

'I don't care,' I snapped, 'if he was a one-eyed, one-legged hobgoblin. He took advantage of you. *He* should be inside.'

'It wasn't his fault, it was mine.'

'Why is it that everything that happens to you is always your fault?'

She stared at me in surprise. 'You're right, Kate,' she said thoughtfully. 'When my sister ran away from home when she was nine I thought that was my fault. When Neil gave up his job I thought that in some way I was to blame for that too.'

'So when you found your son dead in his cot you thought you must have been responsible for that as well?'

She didn't answer; she stood up with her back to me and peeled back the blackout curtains to look outside. I half expected an ARP person to shout, 'Shut that curtain', but all was silent except that it was still raining.

'If I didn't kill him,' said Fran miserably as she turned towards me, 'and I have some doubt now that I did, I still failed to save him. If I hadn't drunk gin that night and then fallen asleep he would still be alive. In a way I'm as guilty as if I had put that pillow over his face.'

'It was Friday night,' I said, 'you'd had a hard week of long hours and regardless of the booze you were exhausted. You're not superhuman.' Then I added, 'In all this you've never once told me where Neil was that night and why in a marriage you don't consider him equally responsible.'

She gave a slight shrug as if dismissing my point of view. 'I don't want to talk about it now.'

'Do you want to talk about your pregnancy?'

'No.'

'Fair enough,' I said. 'Let's get some sleep.'

* * *

At breakfast the next morning we were the first guests up to enjoy the delights of lumpy porridge and scrambled egg made from dried egg powder. The toast was passable. Fran seemed depressed, or was it queasiness that made her reluctant to eat? She managed to eat one slice of toast very slowly. We hardly spoke and I was seriously beginning to wonder if I was the right person to help her. It might be best if I suggested she find someone else.

Mr Martin carried our bags to the car and urged us to tell our friends about the Black Kettle Guest House. We promised we would and I suggested he put it on the internet.

He looked at me aghast. 'You must be joking, Miss Kinsella. Word of mouth is enough. The internet is the work of the devil.'

* * *

St Mary's church was a mere five miles away and although the sky was patchworked in shades of grey the occasional trickle of sunlight escaped. After a couple of miles Fran borrowed my mobile to ring Malcolm. I concentrated on my driving but from Fran's reaction of 'That's wonderful' their conversation seemed to indicate good news. She asked for my mobile number so that he could contact her.

'That's a relief,' she said having finished the call. 'He's found me a furnished cottage to rent for a whole year.'

'Where is it?'

'Bedfordshire somewhere. He's going to ring me later with the details and directions.'

My first reaction was to wonder how far was the hinterland of Norfolk from Bedfordshire? I guessed it was over a hundred miles but until I looked at a map I wouldn't know. I did feel a slight unease generally. I felt responsible for Fran, especially if she did turn out to be pregnant. I couldn't just abandon her now. She was jobless, virtually friendless, pregnant and being pursued, although so far no one had recognized her and with any luck the press wouldn't find her.

St Mary's church was situated on a main road that saw very little traffic and the churchyard had a deserted feel about it. The cemetery itself had one or two graves adorned with fresh flowers, but most had nothing and those that did had arrangements of dried flowers or sad little pots of sodden daffodils. We found Benjamin's grave in a small children's plot at the back of the church. Amongst the other tiny graves, his had the largest headstone of white marble with black lettering. A smattering of sunlight shimmered on the white and black.

Benjamin Rowley
Dearly Beloved son of Neil Rowley
Brother of Fiona
Died tragically aged twenty months

A fresh posy of yellow and white flowers had been placed near to the headstone.

Fran sank to her knees, at first it seemed in prayer, but then she began to shake and after a few moments she gave an anguished scream that I will remember for ever. She began rocking backwards and forwards with tears streaming down her face, making gulping gasping noises and then clutching her stomach. It was as if Benjamin had just died and this was how she might have grieved if the shock had not been so intense.

I let her cry for some time then I put my arms around her and led her back to the car. In the car she cried less but she still couldn't stop. There were no words of comfort I could give her and I didn't try. I handed her a handful of tissues and told her we were driving towards Bedfordshire. I thought the motion of a moving car might be soothing and although my nerves were jangling I had to shut out her despair and concentrate on the road ahead. After a few minutes her sobs grew quieter and she sat fiddling with soggy paper tissues.

'My name wasn't on that headstone,' she said sadly. 'It's as if I didn't exist.'

'That can be changed,' I said. 'Then you'll find peace.'

'I lost my optimism in prison,' she murmured. 'I don't think I'll ever find peace now.'

At that moment my mobile rang from where I'd placed it in the glove compartment. The call was fairly short and Fran repeated the address and directions twice. When she'd finished she replaced the phone. 'Malcolm really is a kind guy,' she said with the hint of a smile. 'He says Oak Leaf Cottage is basic and small but it's warm and cosy and, more to the point, isolated.'

'Where is it exactly?'

'It's on the Rumbold Estate only a mile or so from Woburn. He says it's signposted.'

I carried on driving and decided that when we stopped for lunch I'd look it up on the map. 'Does Malcolm know you're pregnant?' I asked.

It was obvious from her protracted silence that he didn't. 'When are you going to tell the father?'

She shrugged. 'I won't tell either of them for the time being. I think I'm about three months. I could still qualify for an abortion.'

'Is that what you really want?'

'I can't see any other way,' she said miserably.

I wasn't going to try to influence her — it was none of my business — but I knew that for some women early termination was seen as their best option, sometimes their only option. Luckily she didn't seek my opinion. But it did occur to me that if the press found out about her pregnancy they wouldn't leave her alone. And worse, if Social Services got involved they might well try to have the baby taken into care. Somehow I *had* to find out who really did kill Benjamin. If Fran was still considered the killer and she'd carelessly got pregnant on a day out of prison her character would be totally assassinated.

We stopped near Thetford for lunch at a Little Chef. I took one of their free newspapers to read and whilst we waited for our meal I glanced at the front page of the *Sun* newspaper belonging to the man sitting at the next table. *Killer Mother Freed Early* it read and was accompanied by a photograph of Fran looking dull-eyed and grim, which luckily Fran didn't see.

After lunch we paid our bill at the check out and were approaching my car when a voice called out, 'Oi! Ladies!' I turned quickly to see a wiry little man following us. It was the same man who had been reading the *Sun*.

'Car. Quick!' I shouted to Fran.

I accelerated away so fast I didn't have time to look back. I drove on as fast as I dared, convinced that he'd recognized Fran. When I glanced in my mirror to see if he was following there was a green four-wheel-drive on our tail but I couldn't see the driver's face.

CHAPTER SIXTEEN

The four-wheel-drive followed us for a few miles but as I stopped at traffic lights and the car stopped directly behind me I could see the driver was a young blonde woman. I was glad I'd not mentioned my suspicions to Fran; one of us being paranoid was quite enough.

Eventually we reached Woburn and a mile or so from Woburn Sands we found the Rumbold Estate. It was small by stately home standards but the manor house itself was impressive, not only for the building itself but also for the formal gardens that surrounded it. An elderly gardener who was resting on his spade smoking a hand-rolled cigarette directed us to Oak Leaf Cottage. 'You can't miss it,' he said. 'It's about half a mile from the 'ouse on your left and there's a bloody great oak tree in front of it.'

We found the cottage easily enough and if Fran was disappointed she didn't show it. Oak Leaf Cottage was a tiny two-up, two-down dwarfed by the giant oak tree nearby and with rotting window frames and a guttering overflowing with leaves. The key was in the front door and Fran eagerly opened it. Far from being 'warm and cosy' as Malcolm had described it, the front door opened on to the main living room, which struck me as dark and cold. Fran switched on the main overhead light. The lampshade sported cobwebs amongst its yellowing tassels. A coal fire had been laid but not lit and the only furniture was two low armchairs from circa 1930, a drop-leaf table and two wooden chairs. We made our way to the back room to find a kitchen with a butler sink, well stained with age and use, a fat-splattered electric cooker, a small pine table with one carver chair and an elderly fridge.

'All mod cons,' said Fran, sounding quite cheerful.

'You don't have to stay here,' I said. 'I'll ring Hubert and tell him we're coming back.'

'I like it,' she said. 'It needs work but I'll enjoy doing it. I don't have anything else to do . . . until you find Fiona.'

I swallowed hard. Suddenly finding Fiona and finding out who murdered Ben seemed as impossible as climbing a mountain in bedroom slippers. I tried to think positively. Hubert could help, he was good at using the internet and he already had a head start with the name of the employment agency that the nanny had been recruited from.

'Let's look upstairs,' said Fran, sounding quite excited at the prospect.

Up a rather rickety staircase was a tiny hallway with a room either side of it. Both were bedrooms with single beds and small wardrobes. Thin, faded curtains hung at the windows. There was no sign of a bathroom. Downstairs again we opened the kitchen door to find there was a tiny bathroom extension adjacent to the kitchen and next to a small brick coal bunker. It was eccentric but again Fran didn't mind.

'This will be my home for at least a year,' she said. 'It's secluded and safe. What more could I want?'

I could think of a hundred and one things starting with a television, washing machine, central heating, et cetera. 'It's isolated rather than secluded,' I said. 'What about shopping? You'll need a car.'

'I have my own car,' she said. 'Malcolm sorted that for me. He's kept it in a lock-up. He says he'll arrange for a driver to deliver it.' I was impressed; her solicitor was certainly her Man Friday and I recognized in their relationship a similar one to mine and Hubert's — platonic but especially friendly or brotherly or in Hubert's case avuncular.

In the kitchen I inspected supplies. The fridge was full of fresh food, the cupboards were well stocked with dried foods and cans and although we struggled to find matches to light the fire we eventually found those too. Once the fire was lit we waited for the feeble grey smoke to transform itself into glowing coals. It seemed to take for ever but when the fire took hold and the flames began to dance the dull room was instantly transformed.

We were making tea in the kitchen when the phone rang. We had to track the sound but found the phone on the floor behind an armchair. It was Fran's hero, Malcolm. While she was talking I went out to the car to retrieve my mobile phone from the glove compartment. It wasn't there, nor was it in any other part of the car. I went back into the house and checked my handbag and luggage. Our last stop had been the Little Chef and then I realized that the sinister man coming after us waving his arms and shouting 'Oi' was most probably trying to return my mobile phone.

Fran laughed when I told her and she seemed the most relaxed I'd seen her yet. 'He's coming to see me this evening. Isn't that sweet of him?'

It seemed to me that Malcolm's visit would allow me to get back home and start planning this investigation. I wondered now if Fran's pregnancy was a phantom one caused by fear and longing, or if the stress of being released had caused her periods to stop. Either way she hadn't done a pregnancy test so I broached the subject.

'I don't need a testing kit, Kate. I've been pregnant twice and I know how it feels. To put it simply I'm tired all the time, nauseated some of the time and my nipples are tingling.'

There was no arguing with that and an hour later I left. She stood at the front door of the cottage and waved me goodbye. I had the feeling she was glad to see me go.

* * *

I arrived back at Humberstone's late that evening to find Hubert frowning and cross. 'Why didn't you answer your mobile? I've been worried sick.'

'Could we start again, Hubert?' I said. 'How are you, Kate? Have you had a good journey? That would be nice.'

'I'm not doing nice,' he said. 'I'm still doing narked and nasty.'

'Fine. Shall I put the kettle on?'

He calmed down very quickly when I explained that my mobile had been stolen and that I thought we were being followed. It was half true and Hubert had told me half-truths in the past so I didn't feel too guilty.

'I've made some progress,' he said. 'I've found the nanny.'

'How did you do that?'

He smiled smugly. 'The employment agency was reluctant to tell me where Erin was working but I told them under the Child Protection Act they were legally bound to inform an officer of anyone who worked with children and their address.'

'Is that true?'

'No idea but it should be.'

'So where is she working?'

'An address in Hampstead Garden Suburb. A film director with two children under five.'

'I shall have to see her as soon as possible,' I said. 'There's a slight chance that she may still be in contact with Neil and Fiona or she knows more than she told the police.'

'Why rush? Why don't you take a couple of days off?'

'To do what?' I asked.

'Mundane detective work,' he said. 'Plan your investigation.'

'I've done a list,' I said. 'If I work through that and talk to all of Fran and Neil's contacts, sooner or later I'll make a breakthrough.'

'You don't think the police did that at the time of Ben's death?'

'Police investigations grind to a halt if the chief suspect confesses. Why should they waste their time?'

‘You’re such a know-all at times,’ said Hubert, getting irritated. ‘I think you should cultivate one or two of the cops who worked on the case six years ago.’

I observed Hubert’s face. I knew him so well now that when he had discovered a snippet of information and was holding back his expression grew in righteousness. ‘Out with it,’ I said. ‘You know something.’

He smiled. ‘I have found out that a DS, now a DI, did have some doubts at the time. His name is Simon Painter and he’s a bit more local; he’s stationed in Birmingham.’

I looked at Hubert’s face. ‘There’s more, isn’t there?’

He smiled broadly. ‘Yes. He’ll see you tomorrow. An Italian coffee bar, I’ve forgotten the name but it’s on the canal side.’

‘How did you swing that?’ I asked in amazement. ‘And what’s in it for him?’

‘I did tell him you were absolutely gorgeous and that you’d be wearing high heels and a shortish skirt.’

‘You did what!’ I exploded.

‘Now don’t get upset. It’s all in the line of duty.’

‘That’s above and beyond the line of duty. I only do serviceable so he’s going to be a very disappointed fetishist, isn’t he? You found him through one of your pervy shoe chat lines, didn’t you?’

Hubert patted my shoulder. ‘Don’t you see this was meant to be? It’s fortuitous. You need a tame cop. He could be useful for this case and others.’

I took a deep breath. ‘I’ll think about it,’ I said. What had really riled me, although I wasn’t going to admit it to Hubert, was that even looking ‘absolutely gorgeous’ Simon Painter wasn’t going to be a happy, talkative man unless I pulled out all the stops. But I supposed Fran deserved a break and if DI Painter could help me out then I could manage to totter to Birmingham looking cheap.

* * *

The meet had been arranged for midday. I'd taken a taxi from the station and although the day was relatively warm I felt as exposed in a short skirt as if I were wearing a bikini in a supermarket. I'd noticed that women in Longborough rarely showed a leg until temperatures reached eighty degrees Fahrenheit. I was wearing full slap, a skirt that I'd made shorter by turning over the waistband and my hair had been painstakingly teased to look modern and spiky. My shoes, hidden at the back of a wardrobe for years, were black patent leather with four-inch heels. The type you wear once a year and your feet take a week to recover from. I did notice on the train that I had a few covert glances from men and some even managed less covert and more lustful glares.

The spring sunshine after a long dreary winter had brought out shoppers and sightseers and the canal side development had a cheery cosmopolitan atmosphere with people even daring to sit outside the coffee bars. There were two with Italian names and I sashayed past the tables feeling very self-conscious as I scanned faces looking for man with a mildly pervy appearance. One or two men smiled at me, but both were portly and over fifty and not DI material.

I was about to give up when a tall attractive man waved at me with a *Daily Telegraph* and mouthed 'Kate?' I've noticed that my definition of attractive has changed since my twenties became a distant memory. Now a natural set of teeth, no paunch, good posture and a moderate amount of hair counts as attractive. So Simon qualified and as I concentrated on walking tall I smiled at him and he stood and shook my hand. His grip was warm and firm and his smile was disarming. 'Hubert was right,' he said. 'He told me you were absolutely gorgeous.'

'Not so good in flat shoes though,' I said.

'You'd look good in wellies,' he said.

The thought crossed my mind that he could be into rubber too but after all he was only a police contact, I wasn't going to marry him, so I told myself to enjoy the coffee, the sunshine and the information.

He ordered me a Danish pastry and a coffee and insisted it was his treat. I wasn't going to argue and after a short chat on some of the delights of Birmingham I brought up the Rowley case.

'I was at the house when Mrs Rowley was first questioned,' he said.

'What did you think of her?'

'Some of my colleagues thought she was hard and unemotional. She didn't cry or scream. She seemed to me to be in total shock. Numb.'

'Did she seem drunk?' I asked.

'No.'

'Do you think she killed Benjamin?'

He paused. 'She didn't do anything to help herself. "I must have done it," she kept repeating like a mantra as if she were trying to convince herself.'

'If she didn't do it,' I said, 'have you any idea or gut feelings about who might have killed Ben?'

'Oh, yes,' he said. 'The *why* is missing but I do have a prime suspect. Proving it would be impossible though, so it might be as well to let matters stand.'

'I don't agree. Fran needs to know that she's innocent . . . if she is.'

Simon ordered more coffee from a passing waitress and then leant over and whispered in my ear, 'If you agree to see me again, Kate, I'll give you the name of my prime suspect.'

I gave a little shrug as if I were making a small sacrifice. 'You're on. Who is your prime suspect?'

CHAPTER SEVENTEEN

Simon sipped his fresh cup of coffee before answering. 'For some reason the judge and the police seemed to think Neil Rowley was some sort of paragon. He helped out with the children, did a little housework and went out in the evenings two or three times a week. The fact that he had one or two women friends seemed to be accepted as some sort of compensation for having to be at home.'

'So you think Neil killed his only son?' I asked.

'Don't sound so surprised,' he said. 'After all why should Fran have killed *her* only son?'

'From the reports I've read she was angry that Neil wasn't at home, she got drunk and perhaps Ben woke and she silenced him with a pillow. She didn't exactly deny it and she did plead guilty.'

Simon stared at me and I noticed that his brown eyes were framed by long lashes. There was a short pause before he said, 'I was there at the time, Kate, and once the investigating officer was convinced that she was a murderer the investigation ground to a halt. Why put money and resources into a case with a guilty plea?'

'If Neil is your prime suspect, have you any others?'

He smiled. 'One or two. The nanny had an alibi but two of Fran's clients who were violent and abusive did not, but since there was no break-in and the door was locked they were interviewed and eliminated.'

'Did anyone interview Neil's . . . girlfriends?'

'No. They were married women so it was a softly-softly approach.'

It seemed to me that a woman is as likely, perhaps more likely, to kill a baby by suffocation than a man. Horrific stories in the press of men killing young children seemed marked by extreme violence. Maybe a woman was the perpetrator and it would be worth having a chat with Neil Rowley's known extra-marital women friends.

'Would it be possible,' I said to Simon, 'to find me the present addresses of Neil's women?'

'If you have dinner with me tomorrow night then anything is possible,' he said.

'Are high heels mandatory?' I asked.

He looked puzzled. 'Wear whatever you like,' he said. 'Whatever is most comfortable.'

Suddenly I smelt a wind-up. 'Did you contact Hubert via a chat line?'

'No. He actually spoke to a mate of mine in London who gave Hubert my mobile number. I was still interested in the Rowley case and he told me you were great-looking so I had nothing to lose. I'm on annual leave this week anyway.'

'I'll kill him,' I said. 'He told me you were a shoe perv — like him.'

Simon laughed. 'You've got good legs and I am a bit of a leg man but that's as far as it goes.'

I relaxed a bit then, resolving to say nothing to Hubert until I could get my own back with an equally biting wind-up. I liked Simon and there did seem to be a little bit of chemistry going on — not enough to explode a Bunsen burner but enough for a constant simmer.

When I told Simon I planned to go to Hampstead Garden Suburb the next day he offered to go with me.

Although I paused to think about it I delayed too long and he took that as a positive reaction. 'I'll meet you at New Street station at eleven a.m.,' he said. 'We'll make a day of it.'

'I'm not sure,' I said. 'I'm used to working alone most of the time.'

'Investigations don't get solved by one person and I know the background.' He paused. 'And I could gain you access to Mrs Rowley's old home.'

'Throw in regular snacks and it's a deal.'

'You should be in business,' he said. 'See you on the concourse at eleven. Don't be late.'

When I returned to Humberstone's I managed not to say a word to Hubert about his little joke. He did look rather sheepish but he'd cooked a pork stroganoff and opened a good bottle of wine so I quite enjoyed him feeling guilty. I told him I really liked Simon Painter and that I was going to London with him in the morning.

'Just be careful,' he said.

'What of?'

'You might rattle a cage or two. If Fran is innocent someone might want to put a stop to your investigation.'

'I won't be on my own. Simon is tall and quite muscular. He'll take care of me.'

Hubert's face twitched slightly. 'Don't go falling for him. You don't know anything about him.'

'Except his penchant for . . . you know what.'

Hubert swallowed hard and looked about to confess but Jasper interrupted us and Hubert made a hasty exit on the pretext of walkies. That gave me the opportunity to ring Fran.

She sounded fairly upbeat. Malcolm had visited with flowers and champagne and they'd spent hours chatting. 'I feel guilty to have kept him so long because his wife is quite poorly.'

'Where does he live?' I asked.

'North London. He says the house is far too big for them but Maria refuses to move. She's depressed and agoraphobic now and it's having an effect on him. She resents it when he works late but he's planning to send her to an expensive Swiss clinic for a few weeks so he needs to keep his job.'

We chatted for a few minutes about her plans for the cottage but she couldn't contain herself. 'Have you made any progress? Do you know where Fifi is?'

'Everything is in hand,' I said. 'I've got some help from someone you might remember — Simon Painter. He was a Detective Sergeant at the time.'

'Painter,' she repeated. 'Yes, I do remember him. He was more sympathetic than most. Does he think I'm innocent?'

'He thinks it perfectly possible that there was someone else in the house that night.'

Hubert's return signalled an end to our conversation but I did warn Fran that finding Fifi and trying to prove her innocence could take weeks if not months.

* * *

I had never been to Hampstead Garden Suburb before so walking around it was a novelty. The houses and even the trees were extra large and varied in styles, but one thing the residents did all have in common though were long drives, luxury cars in abundant evidence, security gates, cameras, intercoms and a general air of 'Keep out; we're mega rich.'

Delphinium House had its name discreetly on a silver disc high on the front gate. Simon spoke on the intercom. 'Detective Inspector Painter and PI Kinsella to see Erin Gerraty.'

We waited for several minutes until a voice said, 'Come in,' and the automatic gates opened to allow us into the vast lawned frontage and a better view of the Doric columns of the white house.

I half expected a butler to open the front door but instead a young woman in her late twenties holding a toddler in her arms mumbled in the slightest of Irish accents, 'You'd better come in.' She led us through to a large ultra-modern kitchen at the back of the house where she sat the toddler in a high chair and offered him a carrot to chew on. She signalled for us to sit down. 'My boss likes Ferdinand to eat raw food,' she explained. 'He seems to think he's a monkey but when no one's about I slip him a biscuit — it's our little secret, isn't it, Ferdie?' Ferdie threw the carrot on the floor with a mischievous grin.

Erin had long auburn hair tied back loosely, pale skin with a sprinkle of freckles, and green eyes. Slim-waisted with a tiny frame but large breasts, she seemed somehow voluptuous and fragile at the same time. If she'd been a few inches taller Erin could have graced any catwalk.

'What is it you want?' she asked Simon.

'This is Kate,' he said, pushing me forward. 'Fran has taken her on to investigate Ben's death.'

Erin picked up the carrot from the floor and threw it in a waste disposal unit, then she produced a ginger nut biscuit from the pocket of her jeans and placed it in Ferdie's pudgy hand. 'What's to investigate?' she asked as she kissed the top of Ferdie's head. 'I loved that child as if he were my own. I can never forgive Mrs Rowley for what she did.'

'Is there any possibility that there was someone else in the house that evening?'

'No, of course not.'

'Was the back door locked?'

She paused to wipe biscuit from the baby's mouth. 'He's fourteen months old; he's beautiful, isn't he?'

'Was the back door locked?' I repeated.

'Of course it was.'

'When you went out that evening did you leave by the back or the front door?'

'The front door. It was about ten past eight when I left. Mrs Rowley had just come in and she poured herself a gin and tonic and sat down on the sofa.' She paused. 'You know all this, Sergeant.'

'It's Detective Inspector now.'

She nodded, lifted the placid Ferdie from his high chair and sat down with him on her lap.

'I believe you were seeing your boyfriend that evening?' I asked.

'Yes. I spent most evenings at his flat.'

'Are you still seeing him?'

'No.'

'Do you mind me asking why not?'

'After Benjamin was killed I got very depressed. I lost interest in that guy and everything else. I went home to the farm in Ireland for two years and worked as a barmaid. I missed working with children so I came back and Mr Rowley gave me a brilliant reference to get this job. My boss, Giorgio Vincello, is a widower. His wife died of a brain tumour just after Ferdie was born so I've had sole charge of him. I don't get much time off but I love working here.'

'What about Fiona?'

Erin smiled but her eyes were sad. 'She was a sweet child. I did stay on until after the trial but then Mr Rowley said he was thinking of moving and he could manage to look after Fifi on his own. I was upset. I thought that Fifi really needed me. She wasn't the same child after Ben died — very withdrawn, she hardly spoke and she began having nightmares.'

'Were you working for the Rowleys when Fiona was born?' I asked.

She shook her head. 'No. There was a nanny called Tanya. She stayed for a year then left to get married.'

'Do you have her address?'

'No. I'm afraid not.'

'Your boyfriend's address — you do have that?'

'I can tell you where he was living six years ago but I doubt he's still there.'

'I'd appreciate that address and a telephone number.'

'Sure. If you've got a pen and paper I'll write it down.'

As she was writing down the address I said, 'We'll probably get back to you.' For the first time I saw an expression of uncertainty in her eyes. Almost fear.

We made a fuss of Ferdie, thanked Erin and left. As we walked down the drive Simon asked, 'What do you make of her?'

'I'm trying to imagine her six years ago.'

'And?'

'It's just a feeling I have that she was or maybe still is a bit scatty.'

'What do you mean?'

'Her boss doesn't want Ferdie to have biscuits so she gives him biscuits. She comes from rural Ireland and I've heard from Irish nurses I've worked with that in the country doors aren't locked in the day. I can imagine the Rowleys saying to her, "Don't forget to lock the back door" and her forgetting.

'She was never a suspect in my eyes,' said Simon, 'but I never felt she was telling me the whole truth.'

'I do wonder,' I said as the gates opened for us, 'now I've seen how attractive she is, if she was having an affair with Neil. After all, he was at home all day.'

CHAPTER EIGHTEEN

Holland Park for me reflected old money with its grand houses, minimal traffic plus the green space of Holland Park itself. The house that once belonged to the Rowleys had been freshly painted and the frontage had been pot planted with bay plants and miniature pines. It looked smart but unpretentious. The middle-aged woman who opened the door to us had her hair in a towel and looked harassed. 'Oh God, I thought you were the builders. What do want?'

Simon flashed his warrant card, explained the reasons for our visit and that it would be a short one. She shrugged. 'Come on in,' she said. 'Every other bugger does.'

The hallway was dominated by a wide staircase. The kitchen, she informed us, was in the basement.

'You don't need me,' she snapped. 'Just have a poke around. Find your own way. I'm going upstairs to fix my hair.'

Simon of course knew the layout of the house anyway, but I needed to see for myself where Fran once lived and her son had lost his life.

The kitchen was in the throes of a major facelift; units had been ripped out, the floor was covered with debris and the back door was wide open. The garden was mostly hidden now by several planks of wood, an old fireplace and the remains of the kitchen units. Surrounding the garden was a wall about six feet high. The end of the garden was enclosed by a heavy oak door with bolts top and bottom and a keyhole with a key in situ.

'Where does that lead to?' I asked.

'It's a service road,' said Simon. 'I expect the builders use it. A small van could easily be backed up for deliveries.'

'If anyone was leaving the house would there be any advantage in leaving by the back entrance?'

He thought for a moment. 'It cuts off walking round the block and there's another cut through point which leads to a bus stop.'

'Do you know if Erin took the bus that night?'

'No, but I could find out.'

We toured the rest of the house but by then builders had arrived and trying to imagine the house as it had been that night was too difficult for someone with my degree of spatial incompetence. My overall impression, though, was of a very large house. Somewhere on one of the three floors, plus an attic, someone could have hidden for a day if not longer.

We crept out as the workmen plugged in their radio and blasted us out with Radio One. 'Right,' said Simon. 'Let's make our way to Erin's old boyfriend's place.'

'Have you met him before?' I asked.

'Just the once, to corroborate Erin's alibi.'

'What's he like?'

'You'll have to make up your own mind.'

I was expecting a scruffy bed-sit but the house, although smaller than the Rowleys', was just as impressive and so too was the gold plaque fixed to the wall. Desmond Hallam was a GP.

'At least he should be in,' I said.

His young receptionist, once told of our mission, disappeared into his consulting room and returned seconds later to say we could go straight in. It was the shortest wait I'd ever had in a GP's surgery.

Dr Hallam was at least fifty with thin grey hair, heavy framed glasses, large ears and fleshy lips. He wasn't in the least attractive and taking off six years would have made no difference. He stood up to greet us, shook both our hands and appeared willing, even keen, to talk to us.

'Erin was, I have to admit,' he said, 'the love of my life. How is she?'

'She's fine,' said Simon.

'Is she married?'

Simon shook his head.

'I wanted to marry her. Did she tell you that?'

'No,' said Simon. 'She said that after Ben's tragic death she became depressed and you two grew apart.'

'She grieved for Ben; that was natural. She loved that child as if he were her own. Her depression was totally normal.'

'How often did you see her?' I asked.

'Three times a week, sometimes more. She'd come here. I live above the shop. Sometimes we'd eat out but usually she had supper with the children.'

I hesitated. 'As a couple you seem a little unlikely,' I said.

'I suppose you mean the age difference. It didn't bother us. Erin likes older men. She was very mature for her age.'

'Did you see her at weekends?' Simon asked.

He shook his head. 'She worked at weekends.'

'Were you jealous of the children?' I asked.

'Jealous?' he murmured in response. 'I did resent them a little. She was very attached to the family.'

'So when Ben was killed did you see that as an opportunity for her to leave the Rowleys?'

He took off his glasses and stared at me. 'What are you getting at? Mrs Rowley killed her son, she pleaded guilty, went to prison — end of story.'

'We're working on the supposition that she didn't kill Benjamin, therefore someone else must have.'

'So I'm the fall guy, am I?' said Hallam angrily.

'No,' said Simon calmly. 'We're just making preliminary enquiries.'

'Well, stuff your enquiries. I'd like you to leave now.'

'Dr Hallam,' I said in my most soothing tone, 'we're only trying to eliminate people so that we don't have to keep returning to you to answer yet more questions. If you help us now we won't need to come back.'

He slipped on his glasses and shrugged. 'What else do you want to know?'

'Do you think that Erin could have been seeing another man—?'

'Don't be ridiculous,' he interrupted. 'She was a good Catholic girl.'

'Did she go to Mass?'

'Yes. Every Sunday.'

'Which church?'

'St Mary's, I think. We didn't discuss religion.'

'But are you totally convinced she wasn't having sex with anyone else?' I paused. 'Someone such as Neil Rowley?'

If Dr Hallam had a panic button he would have pressed it then. His grey eyes glowed angrily. 'You may have met Erin but you didn't know her. She was pure and innocent.'

'But she was having sex with you two or three times a week.'

'For God's sake, woman. Not all relationships are based on sex. We didn't have sex. We . . .' He faltered. 'I just loved her.' His voice broke and suddenly I felt very sorry for him. He loved too much — or maybe worshipped was a better description.

We left Dr Hallam sitting at his desk with his head in his hands. Simon and I were silent as we walked towards Notting Hill Gate tube station. Passing a pub where a few brave souls sat outside drinking he said, 'We need a drink and a discussion about what to do next.'

The pub was busy and noisy but neither of us minded. We managed to find a corner seat and Simon drank beer and ate steak and kidney pie while I ate a modest burger with salad and drank lager.

'Dr Hallam's revelation came as a surprise to me,' he said. 'Everyone just assumed they were bonking.'

'What was Erin doing at weekends? That's what interests me.'

'Speak to Fran. She might know.'

'I expect Erin was friendly with other nannies,' I said. 'That might be an avenue worth exploring.'

After I'd been fed and watered I began to feel both sleepy and dispirited. Murder throws up so many contacts, so many people who impinged on the Rowleys' life. Fran had spent most of her life at work and I thought a visit to her office might be our next step.

Luckily Simon agreed and we made our way by tube to the offices of Hunter, Hunter and Blaze. By the time we arrived it was nearly five p.m. Although it was one of the leading law firms in London their offices were not that impressive, the stuccoed walls, once cream or white, were now more nicotine-coloured. The reception area was as full of potted plants as a conservatory and the receptionist, Rebecca, may have watered the plants but her red talons and white hands proved she was no gardener. She smiled broadly at us, and even our explanation of the reason for our visit didn't interrupt her smile. Simon asked to see Malcolm Talgarth.

'I'm sorry, he's not in the building at the moment. I'm sure the senior partner, Mr Valentine, will see you.'

She rang him on the internal phone and, still smiling, nodded to us to go up. 'Fourth floor,' she said. 'The lift is on the right.'

The lift was narrow and ancient, the sort whose internal door you have to close yourself and then clank to the floors rather than glide. Mr Valentine had his office door open and stood to greet us. Mid-fifties, tall and angular, he wore rimless glasses and his rumpled grey suit, slightly wonky tie and shaggy grey hair curling above his collar gave the impression of a man much pressed for time and a little past caring.

'Do sit down,' he said. 'How can I help?'

'We wanted to have a word with Malcolm Talgarth but he isn't in the office.'

'No. Unfortunately is wife rather ill so we're not sure when he'll be back.'

'Were you senior partner when Francesca Rowley worked here?' I asked.

'I was indeed.'

'What was your impression of Mrs Rowley?'

'Solid woman, absolutely. Hard worker.'

'Did she get on well with her colleagues?'

'I heard nothing to the contrary although there's always some backbiting.'

'What about?'

'That she always got the celebrity clients but she acquired those through dint of hard work and being a very patient listener. She was also simpatico.'

'We did hear,' said Simon, 'that there were occasional violent incidents with one or two of her clients.'

'Yes, that was unfortunate but we live in a violent society and emotions are heightened by the trauma of divorce. I myself specialize in company law — far less stressful.'

'So Fran was stressed?' I remarked, trying to sound casual.

'Averagely so, I suppose, although . . .' He broke off.

'Although what?' I asked.

'The last couple of weeks she was here she did say she thought she had a stalker. It seems she had a few silent phone calls and she had the feeling that she was being followed.'

'Did she suspect anyone?'

'No. She was very stoical about it. Matter-of-fact.'

'I know Fran pleaded guilty at her trial,' I said, 'but in your opinion was she capable of killing her own child?'

His gaze at me just stopped short of being a stare. 'Oh, I'm sure she was. Yes, she could well have done it.'

CHAPTER NINETEEN

I was so surprised I didn't know what to say. Simon noticed the look on my face and took over. 'Would you explain that, sir, because I don't remember any comments like that being made at the time of our initial enquiries.'

'I can't remember my exact words but certain incidents came to light that showed Mrs Rowley was not always as well controlled as she appeared.'

Having now gathered my wits I said, 'Could you explain that?'

'I wasn't there at the time so it's purely rumour and gossip and no one in the firm told the police. It reflects badly on the firm. We do have a very respectable image.'

'What the hell did she do?'

'She attacked a client.'

'Why?'

'I've no idea.'

'No one asked her?'

'Of course, but she didn't want to talk about it. She was obviously upset so it was hushed up, the client was paid compensation and Mrs Rowley was admonished and fined.'

'When did this happen?' asked Alex.

Bernard Valentine looked away as if embarrassed. 'It happened on the Monday of the week in which she killed her son.'

'Were there any other . . . incidents?' I asked.

'She did smash two mugs against a wall in the kitchen.'

'I suppose that happened in the same week?'

He nodded. 'She was on the edge, I suppose.'

'How many hours was she working?' I asked.

'I've no idea. We all work long hours. Probably a twelve-hour day and sometimes she took work home.'

'Not conducive to mental health then,' I said between gritted teeth.

'In my opinion,' he said, 'and I keep this to myself, women with children shouldn't be in the workplace. She put her career first and obviously we benefited from that but her husband and children couldn't fail to suffer.'

Anger made my voice croaky. 'I suppose it never occurred to you to try to make her work life a little easier?'

'I'm a businessman. I can't afford slackers or emotional outbursts. She joined us knowing it would be hard work but for which she was very well paid. And she did prove she could do the job, but like many married women with children they do fail in the long term for many reasons. Men have what I'd call focused drive.'

I took a deep breath. 'Do you know what I'd like to do with your "focused drive"?' I paused as Simon nudged me but I wasn't going to be stopped. 'I'd stick it up your arse.'

Mr Valentine blinked. 'What did I say?' he asked in surprise at my outburst. 'I'm only saying it as it is.'

I turned on my heel and left the room. I was incandescent. As we waited for the lift Simon put his arm around me. 'Calm down, Kate. He's not the only man to think like that.'

I took a deep breath. 'I'm beginning to think,' I said, 'that Fran, being so stressed and exhausted, *did* kill Ben.'

'You're overreacting,' said Simon, guiding me into the lift as if I'd suddenly become frail and in need of assistance. 'Let's get back to Longborough and I'll see what I can find out about Neil Rowley's whereabouts.'

On the train back, which was half an hour late, I didn't feel like talking so I observed our fellow passengers then closed my eyes and pretended to be asleep. All around me were tired, hollow-eyed commuters, some valiantly still doing paperwork, others falling asleep over the latest must-read novel. How did they do it day after day? One day in London was more than enough for me. I found the traffic noise and general air of frenetic activity wearing. Everyone, except for down and outs and beggars, gave me the impression that their time was ultra precious, as if somehow a life lived slowly was of less importance. Why else would a lunch hour face lift be such a good idea? Waste a whole day on a face lift? That seemed to indicate that the customer was far too important to have time to spare.

In Longborough people looked for ways to pass time slowly. They stopped to chat about the weather or the newest vicar or the graffiti. Those who had jobs knew they would never take them to dizzy heights; those who were retired were glad they were no longer working and if they had crow's feet, who cared? With eyesight failing most people seemed forever young and life's pleasures could then take over. There was no need to seek out a gym or be denied an extra sprinkling of salt or a cream cake. What was the point of worrying any more? I'd reached that stage in my thirties. I was getting older and although the Zimmer frame was a long way off, I liked the slow pace of Longborough. Or was I simply too lazy to bother about the health and anti-aging fascists spreading their propaganda in the media? Even without rushing life was too short to watch alfalfa sprouts grow unless it was purely for the joy of seeing them grow. Fun, pleasure, growing older had to be put on hold for as long as possible. Pensions had to be paid for and 'work until you drop' had become the new mantra. As if staying healthy, thinking young, looking young would somehow keep the cogs of capitalism moving.

Fran, in her attempts to pay the mortgage and keep her husband in the lifestyle that she provided him with, had taken on the problems of others and failed to see her own life was in crisis. Guilty or innocent she still needed help. The media had crucified her and yet her husband's failings were tolerated as if he were a dependent teenager.

After my musings I did drift off to sleep and Simon woke me to say, 'This is Birmingham. I'll phone you.' He kissed me briefly on the lips, so briefly that in my post-sleep fuzz I almost missed it.

Hubert and Jasper were pleased to see me. Jasper, as excited as ever, wanted a cuddle and even Hubert gave me a hug. 'I've only been to London,' I said.

'With a strange man,' replied Hubert, arming himself with a pair of oven gloves.

'You introduced us,' I said.

'Maybe that was a mistake.'

'Why, because I like him?'

'No. I think it's too soon after David to fall head over heels.'

'You're exaggerating,' I said. 'One trip to London wouldn't even make me head over heels with George Clooney.'

Hubert went to the oven and peered inside. 'I'll serve up and you can tell me what you found out.'

The Irish stew was delicious and Jasper, who we both fed surreptitiously under the table, enjoyed it too.

'Have you any leads?' asked Hubert, unable to wait any longer.

I told him about seeing Erin the nanny and her ex-boyfriend.

'What was he like?'

'A middle-aged GP and according to him they weren't having sex.'

Hubert made tutting noises. 'What is the world coming to?'

'It's not a joke,' I said, 'because if she wasn't having sex with him, who was she having sex with?'

'She could be doing without, like you.'

I didn't answer that and began clearing the table.

But Hubert was in inquisitive mode. 'If she was having sex with someone else then why was she seeing the doctor?'

I paused, plate in hand, about to put it in the dishwasher. 'You've just made a very good point. What would I do without you?'

'What did I say?'

'According to the doc Erin is as pure as holy water, goes to church and seemingly doesn't bonk, at least not with him. So she must have been fulfilling some need three times a week.'

'Companionship?' suggested Hubert.

'I was thinking more in terms of his being a supplier.'

It took a moment for Hubert's terminals to spark. 'You mean he was supplying her with drugs?'

'It's a possibility.'

'Does she look like an addict?'

'Not all addicts are scruffy and unwashed.'

'How are you going to find out?'

'One thing at a time,' I said. 'I'm having trouble sorting out priorities at the moment.'

If I was truthful I already felt that I'd taken on a case that was far beyond my capabilities.

'What about Fran's girl friends?' Hubert's question was pertinent but as the only person who visited her or contacted her in prison was her solicitor friend I felt they must have abandoned her for a reason and I wasn't sure I wanted to hear any more negative reactions.

'I may have misjudged Fran's personality,' I said. 'According to the senior partner Bernard Valentine, in the week before Ben died Fran was behaving . . . erratically.'

'So are you saying she did kill Ben?'

I shook my head feeling despondent. 'There is something else . . .' I paused. There was no other way to put it but bluntly. 'Fran is pregnant.'

Hubert eyes bulged. 'How?'

'The natural way,' I said. 'Her probation officer took her on a day out to help her adjust to life outside prison and he took advantage of her.'

Hubert stared at me. 'The more I hear about Mrs Rowley the less I like the whole set up. I think she's taking you for a ride. She wants to find her daughter, which is natural, but is she stable? Would her daughter be in danger?'

'OK, she had sex with a stranger. If I'd been in prison for six years I might well do the same.'

'Would you then say the man took advantage of you?'

'Fran blamed herself, not him.'

'That's something, I suppose. Even so, be warned by Uncle Hubert — I think she's bad news.'

I couldn't bring myself to admit to him that maybe I'd totally misjudged Fran's character and that he was right. After all, a week at Peace Haven didn't mean I'd delved into her psyche. She'd just been released from prison, and I hadn't been planning to use my brain for anything more than enjoying a massage or two. If I'd been seeing a man in the romantic sense I'd want at least six months to get to know him. Even then logic and rationality can fly out of the bedroom window when faced with pure lust. My trouble being I hadn't experienced pure lust for a very long time. Fran had a healthy sex drive — that didn't make her a murderer — and she could be spirited, but that just made her human. I decided I would continue with the investigation and keep an open mind.

A little later I went to my office and rang Fran. She took ages to answer the phone. When she did eventually answer I asked, 'How are you coping?'

'Quite well,' she said. 'But then I do have help. Malcolm is staying for a couple of days and he's doing all sorts of odd jobs for me.'

'Doesn't his wife mind?'

'No. She's staying with her mother for a few days.'

'I see,' I said. 'Have you had any morning sickness?'

She paused. 'I'm feeling fine.' So guarded was her response I knew he was in the same room.

'Give me a ring when he's gone, won't you?'

'Of course I will, Kate. Is there any news?'

'It's early days. Take care of yourself.'

I was about to put the phone down when she said in a whisper, 'Malcolm says I'm still in danger. He's received threatening letters to be forwarded to me. He wants me to leave here . . . What should I do?'

CHAPTER TWENTY

I needed a moment to think but Fran didn't give me a chance. 'I've got to go,' she whispered. The phone call left me disconcerted. I needed to talk to her face to face; not only did we need to discuss my meeting with Bernard Valentine but also her pregnancy. The threatening letters were a worry but if she was careful and stayed put I reasoned the sender might eventually lose interest.

I was daunted by my list of people to see. I wanted results quickly but I knew I should take my time and be methodical. Finding her sister came top of the list because she might well know where her niece was living. *Family first* would be my motto but it would mean leaving Longborough again and I guessed Hubert might disapprove.

I caught up with him in the lounge. He sat, feet up, fast asleep on the sofa with Jasper lying by his side. Both of them were snoring and I couldn't bring myself to wake them up.

In the morning over breakfast I told Hubert that I planned to visit Fran if her solicitor friend had returned home and then base myself at a hotel in London for a while.

'I'll find you somewhere to stay on the internet,' he said. 'I might take a trip to London myself if we're not too busy.'

I knew he wanted to be involved but Simon was the man with the contacts and experience of the case. He hadn't rung me and although I could have rung him he was meant to be on annual leave so I reckoned he could probably do with a rest.

'I'm taking the car,' I said.

'Don't try driving around central London,' warned Hubert. 'There's the congestion charge and parking to worry about.'

He was in anxious mode now and he rushed off to sort me out some accommodation on the internet. I began packing and by the time I returned to the kitchen Hubert was looking smug.

'I've found you a nice place,' he said. 'Ivy Court Hotel, near Russell Square and it's cheap.'

'Is that its only recommendation?'

'No. It's females only. You'll be safe there.'

'Oh, good,' I said. 'I'd hate to think marauding men might be trying to share my bed.'

Hubert flashed me one of his looks that suggested if I said any more I wouldn't be the recipient of his good nature or his delicious full English breakfasts. So I thanked him and told him I thought a girls-only hotel was a great idea. He didn't look that convinced any more.

'What time are you going?' he asked.

'After I've rung Fran to make sure Malcolm has gone.'

'Ring me when you get there,' he said. 'I've had a premonition that something nasty is going to happen.'

'I didn't know you believed in premonitions. Next you'll be telling me you believe in the afterlife and reincarnation.'

'At my age I rule nothing out but my premonition was that someone you knew died.'

'You really are the voice of doom,' I said. 'You're making me twitchy and being twitchy is the last thing a PI needs.'

'Don't say you haven't been warned.'

I went to ring Fran from my office before the tetchiness between Hubert and me became a full-blown row. Malcolm had gone to work and Fran was looking forward to seeing me. She sounded less anxious now and I explained that I'd only be staying one night and that I'd be continuing my investigation in London.

'I just want to see Fiona again,' she said plaintively. 'I don't care about my guilt or innocence.'

'I care,' I said. 'Your life can change if we find the murderer. If we don't you'll always be looking behind you — you won't be able to move on.'

I'd just put the phone down when my mobile rang. The mobile was courtesy of Hubert, with a cock-a-doodle-do ring tone. It was Simon. He didn't sound very upbeat and after a few pleasantries he told me he couldn't see me for a while as his mother was ill. Alarm bells trilled loudly in my ear. 'Is she in hospital?' I asked.

'No. She has carers who visit but I live with her so most of the responsibility is mine.'

I sighed inwardly. I supposed an ailing mother was one better than him being married but my initial burst of enthusiasm was beginning to fade as fast as the sun sets in the tropics.

'I have got an address for you,' he said. 'There's a Giles Skipton listed at . . . have you got a pen?'

I hurriedly found a pen and wrote down the address. They were living in St Albans. Very close to where Fran was now staying. Already I had visions of a happy reunion.

'I'll ring you,' said Simon.

I wondered if he actually would but at least Fran's sister's whereabouts was a start — and you can't have everything.

* * *

Fran had made changes to the cottage. There were fresh flowers in every room and in the kitchen the units had been given a fresh coat of white paint.

'I didn't do it,' she said. 'Malcolm did. He's very handy.' With her freshly washed hair and careful make-up

Fran looked younger and prettier. The effects of prison were beginning to disappear although there was still a slight pallor.

She'd made soup and sandwiches for lunch and I waited for the right moment to tell her about her sister living nearby. After musing over it through the soup course I decided it wasn't such a good idea. After all, her sister had rejected Fran's communications for six years and I didn't want to risk her being rejected again until I found out more about Ben's real murderer.

'I want you to be totally honest with me,' I said out of the blue.

Fran looked up in surprise. 'I want to know more about Neil and his women friends.'

'There isn't much to say,' she said briskly. 'I was a fool to have stayed with him but I loved him. I really did.'

'That isn't the point, Fran. Who were these women and why didn't your defence team make more of his adulterous behaviour?'

'I didn't have a "defence team", as you put it. Malcolm gave me guidance but I made that choice. I didn't want Neil's reputation tarnished in any way. You see, I knew I would go to prison and if it seemed that Neil was an unreliable father I was worried that Fifi might have been taken into care.' She paused. 'It does happen. Even to the middle classes.'

'I believe he was involved with two women. Do you know who they are?'

'I have my suspicions.'

'Yes?'

'They are both married women and anyway so much time has gone by.'

'I'll be very discreet.'

Reluctantly she wrote down their names and last known addresses on a scrap of paper and handed it to me. 'Tell me about these women,' I said.

'The husbands were older friends of Neil's. Before Ben was born we had a dinner party about once a month and three or four couples were always invited.'

'When did you start to get suspicious?'

She frowned. 'Sara Nelson told me once, after she'd had a few drinks, that Neil was the "most divine man she'd ever met". And Natalie Lincoln was always thrusting her factory-produced breasts at him.'

'That doesn't necessarily indicate an affair as such.'

'I realize that, but neither Sara nor Natalie earned a living. Although their body maintenance programmes were time consuming they could have managed to fit in a quickie with Neil between visits to the gym, the beautician, the hairdresser, the cosmetic surgeon and their therapists.'

'You don't rate them then?' I said with a smile.

'Made it obvious, have I?' she said with a little grin. 'It's true I despise them but the final results of all that pampering were evident not only in their looks but in their confidence . . .' She paused. 'Both their husbands were the most boring old farts who, while striving to make more and more money for their wives to spend, failed to realize that they were not the objects of their wives' desire.'

'So you suspected that Neil was having lunchtime trysts with both women?'

'Yes. Under a pretext, of course.'

'Which was?'

'He painted them. Nudes and the occasional portrait.'

'Did Erin tell you?'

'No, she didn't. I went up to the attic and saw the paintings.'

'Were they any good?'

'He made them look like perfect androids. And of course the reconstructed duo's husbands loved their wives and the paintings enough to buy them. Neil bought an Aston Martin with the money.'

'Don't you hate him?' I asked.

She shook her head slowly as if it were a debatable point. 'I despise him. He had everything — a devoted wife, wonderful children, a good standard of living — but it wasn't enough.'

'At least you're not blaming yourself.'

'I did, still do. If I'd stayed at home and been dependent on him I think he would have felt more manly, more in control. You see, he knew I could manage without him.'

Fran had given me something to think about, but what could I glean from the fact that he was having sex with two women? Where the hell did Benjamin's death fit in?

'Do you think either Sara or Natalie were in love with Neil?'

She smiled. 'I don't know for sure but I would think it very unlikely. Neil couldn't give them the money they needed to keep their youthful looks. They were using him for sex and to fuel their confidence. To be honest, I think they pitied me. I was poor Fran, hard-working and serviceable but not adored or pampered.'

'So I could rule them out as suspects?'

'What would be their motive? After all, they were self-obsessed and not deranged.'

My one thought at that moment was who the hell *could* have a motive strong enough to kill a child? But it would still be worth tracing them just in case they knew where Neil and Fiona were now living.

I slipped the addresses into my purse and took a deep breath before telling Fran about my visit to her senior partner.

'My last week there was awful,' she said.

'In what way?'

'A mad client. I get used to abuse because divorce and money rakes up just about the most stressful, nasty, sometimes evil emotions that can be imagined. Anyway, I can't go into details but his wife was making allegations about his behaviour. I merely asked if it was true and he began hitting his wife. She was cowed but I wasn't. I kicked him in the balls so hard that he keeled over.'

'Good for you.'

'The firm didn't think so. When he began making threats about suing me for assault, Bernard Valentine paid him off.'

'And I hear you smashed some mugs too.'

'Yes. I was het up. They were both cracked and I threw them against the wall.'

I didn't think any of this added up to a person capable of killing their child. Undoubtedly she was stressed and had needed a little alcohol to unwind, but I thought in her position I'd need a vat.

Later we watched an old black and white film on television and during the advert break I asked Fran about her female colleagues.

'They were nice enough,' she said. 'There were two other solicitors and a trainee. They were keen, single and focused. They discussed films and nightclubs and weekends in Paris. I wanted to chat about nappy rash and potty training. We had nothing in common.'

'And what about Malcolm?'

She smiled. 'He was always a good listener. He'd even pop out for sandwiches for me. He worried that I didn't eat enough.'

'Did you ever meet his wife?'

'No. He seemed . . . sad, I suppose, when he talked about her. She's a manic depressive.'

We went back to watching the film which was deteriorating from poor to dire. The film certainly couldn't keep my attention and my thoughts drifted back to Malcolm, the one person besides me who didn't think she was guilty. Or was he in love with her, and in fact believed the opposite but wanted to help her in any way he could?

'Have you seen these threatening letters?' I asked Fran.

'No,' she said, still watching one of the worst films ever made.

'Has Malcolm taken them to the police?'

'No, he's destroyed them.'

'Why?'

'He doesn't want me to be upset by them and he says the police haven't got the time or the inclination to deal with it.' She finally looked away from the screen. 'And I did leave their new model witness protection scheme so I'm definitely persona non grata now.'

'You told me on the phone,' I said, 'that Malcolm wanted you to leave here. Where does he think you should go and why does he think this cottage isn't safe?'

'He says it's just a gut feeling.'

'I have a gut feeling too: that someone at your office knows he's rented this place.'

CHAPTER TWENTY-ONE

'You might be right, Kate,' said Fran, switching off the television. 'But there's no one I know at the office who would write threatening letters. They may not be friends but my colleagues were decent people and I didn't have any enemies there.'

Except for Bernard Valentine, I thought. I needed to know if any of her original colleagues still worked at Hunters. I jotted down the various names Fran gave me and reluctantly she also gave me the names of a few obnoxious clients including the man she had dealt with so appropriately.

In bed that night I lay awake fretting about how best to tackle the investigation. Should I be concentrating on Fran's closest contacts or listening to character assassinations from people who really didn't know her? But of course I didn't know her that well either. Her sister, I decided, must be my first priority in the morning. I had her address and St Albans wasn't far. I fell asleep feeling quite optimistic.

In the morning Fran questioned me about who I planned to see that day but I was non-committal. I didn't want to raise her hopes that there would be a swift outcome to the case. I knew finding her daughter was Fran's priority but proving her innocence was mine. Once I had the evidence — if there was any after so long — Fran could begin to live a normal life.

* * *

The address Simon had given me for Giles Skipton was a small detached house on the outskirts of St Albans. It didn't look expensive but I knew that house prices in St Albans, being so close to London, were extremely high. I rang the doorbell long and hard but there was no reply. Three houses away I found a young mother outside her front garden struggling to open her gate with one hand and control a baby buggy in the other. As I held the gate open for her, she smiled.

'Thanks. I've only been walking to quieten him down. It's the only time he sleeps.' She was in her late twenties, wearing jeans and a black denim jacket with black shadows under her eyes to match. 'I've been to number seven,' I said, 'looking for the Skiptons.'

She raked her hand through her lank hair and thought for a moment. 'I don't know his name but he's middle aged. I think he works in London. I've seen him coming back quite late sometimes.' She smiled wryly. 'I've only seen him because I've been trying to get the baby asleep by walking him round the block.'

'Do you see his wife?' I asked.

'I've never seen a woman there but I've only lived here a few months.'

I thanked her, got into my car and tried to phone Simon but his mobile was switched off. Then I tried Hubert but he wasn't answering either. Disappointed, I drove towards London, eventually parked my car, a mile away from Southgate tube station, and travelled into central London in relative non-rush-hour comfort.

At a cafe near Fran's old office I ordered a cappuccino and a cheese and ham panini after getting palpitations at the cost. No wonder people complained that living in central London was stressful. Anyway, when it arrived it tasted fine and on a full stomach and with a more stable blood sugar I felt better able to deal with Bertram Valentine — if, that is, I couldn't avoid him.

There was a new receptionist at the desk. Smart but not red-taloned, she was in her late thirties and her name badge read Susan White.

'Hi,' I said cheerfully. 'I haven't got an appointment but I've come to see Malcolm Talgarth.'

'I'm sorry,' she said, 'he's on compassionate leave. He rang us this morning to say his wife was worse and he wouldn't be coming back for the foreseeable future.'

'Oh. I was hoping to ask him about a friend of mine — Fran Rowley. I've been abroad, we lost touch and I know she used to work here.'

'You knew Malcolm as well?' she asked with a tinge of suspicion.

'No, I don't know him at all; an acquaintance mentioned him and the name of the firm so I thought I'd give it a try as I'm in London. I didn't think Fran would still be here. The last I heard she'd had a daughter called Fiona.'

'You don't know about Fran being in prison?' she whispered as someone entered reception.

'Prison?' I gasped in mock surprise.

'I'm due for a break soon,' she said. 'If you wait outside I'll meet you in ten minutes.'

Luckily it wasn't raining but I felt somewhat conspicuous hanging around outside. When Susan did come out she ushered me away from the office into an alleyway where she took a packet of cigarettes from her pocket, offered me one which I declined, lit it and took a deep drag. 'That's better,' she sighed. 'Smokers are the new lepers but I'm weak and I've tried to give up several times. One day I'll succeed . . . Now, let me tell you about Fran.'

She told me what I already knew but I pretended to be horrified, surprised and sad all at the same time. My performance was worthy of an Oscar, I thought.

'Were you surprised?' I asked.

'Surprised? I was really shocked. She adored both her children. She must have been totally unbalanced at the time.'

'Did her colleagues stick by her?'

A sudden gust of wind blew her cigarette smoke in my face. 'I'm ashamed to stay no one did . . . well, except Malcolm. We didn't know what to say to her.'

'Good old Malcolm,' I said.

'He's a nice guy; we weren't surprised he helped in Fran's defence. He wanted her to plead temporary insanity but she refused.'

'So Fran is out of prison now?' I queried.

'That's what I read in the papers.'

'Where's she living? I'll go and see her.'

Susan shrugged and took a long suck on her cigarette. 'I've no idea.'

'What about Neil and poor Fiona?'

'No one knows where they are. Neil was devastated to lose his son. At the funeral he was in a terrible state. I heard it rumoured that he was so angry with Fran he'd wanted to kill her.'

'What a terrible tragedy,' I murmured.

'Yeah. I really liked Fran. She always seemed cheerful and pleasant but you can never *really* know someone, can you?'

'No, that's true.' I paused. 'About Malcolm — what's wrong with his wife?'

She shrugged. 'No idea. But I expect he'll be able to help you find Fran. I know his address if you want it, because I forwarded some mail for him today.'

'That's great,' I said, jotting down his address as she gave it to me. 'I'll pay him a visit.'

Susan returned to her desk nicotine fuelled and immediately it began to rain so I treated myself to a taxi. Traffic was comparatively light and although I tried to relax and plan the questions I wanted to ask Malcolm I found myself simply gazing through the taxi window, lulled by the London sights.

The house was a large Edwardian semi with ivy creeping up the walls and a front door with a stained-glass window decorated with yet more ivy. The front garden had been paved over and the sash windows were freshly painted in dark green. There were no pot plants or hanging baskets and the porch was devoid of colour. Especially in the rain my overall impression was that the house itself had less than lively occupants and bordered on the gloomy.

Malcolm opened the door. I'd tried to picture him in my mind several times, and somehow I'd expected a round-faced kindly looking guy. In the dog world he'd have been a Labrador. Instead he was tall, lean verging on thin, his hair was beginning to grey, he wore rimless glasses and a distracted look. Rather than being dressed, he seemed to have fallen into his clothes; his trousers hung loosely, and his sweater, once black, was now a thin and faded grey. As a dog he would have been the stray mongrel in the dog pound that no one wanted. As a man he looked like a bachelor in need of a little wifely nagging.

'Come on in,' he said. 'I've heard a lot about you, Kate. You're been very kind to Fran so I'm delighted to meet you.' He spoke softly with a slight accent, perhaps from Devon or Cornwall I guessed.

He led me through to his spacious kitchen and immediately put the kettle on. 'My wife Maria is upstairs in bed,' he explained. 'She's often in bed.'

'Have you called the doctor?'

He managed a half smile. 'Many times. She has a private psychiatrist I call regularly but apart from medication there's nothing anyone can do. Mental illness is the real Cinderella of the NHS.'

I agreed with that as he made a pot of tea and offered me chocolate biscuits. Then he carefully prepared a tray. 'I'll take this up to her,' he said with a smile. 'Help yourself to tea.'

He was gone several minutes while I drank tea and I wandered about the kitchen. On the window sill, overlooking a straggly high-fenced garden, were a bunch of white lilies in a black vase and their sweet, rather sickly smell reminded me of Fran's cottage. Malcolm had obviously bought a job lot.

When he came back into the kitchen he looked anxious. He sat down, or rather he slumped. 'You seem to be having a difficult time,' I said.

He rested his chin on his right hand as if trying to keep his head above water. 'These last few weeks she's been worse than ever. Sometimes she gets up at night and wanders around the house as if she's looking for something. I don't know what to do about it.'

I didn't have an answer so I stayed silent.

'You've come to talk about Fran,' he said, 'not listen to my problems.'

I smiled and nodded. 'You've been so kind to Fran, and I wanted to ask your advice.'

'What about?'

'Her priority right now is seeing her daughter again. Mine at the moment is trying to prove her innocence. How best should I proceed?'

He gazed at me steadily. 'What about the threatening letters?'

'Crackpots who merely want to scare her.'

'You haven't read them so how can you judge?'

'Fair point,' I agreed. 'Could I see them?'

'I've destroyed some but others are with the police. They are investigating.'

I let the threatening letters issue drop because in my opinion Fran was perfectly safe at the moment.

'Have you any idea where Neil and Fiona might have gone?' I asked.

He shrugged. 'None at all except that I don't think Neil would retreat to the country. He's not the type.'

'You knew him?'

'Oh, yes. I'd met him. He liked casinos, theatres, expensive restaurants.'

'You don't sound as if you approved of him.

'I didn't; he wasn't good enough for Fran.'

'Is there anyone at all you could possibly suspect of killing Ben?' I asked.

His reply was slow and measured. 'Fran pleaded guilty. My aim was to find a barrister who would plead mitigating circumstances. In that I failed her. The barrister I chose was a mistake; he was an incompetent blustering idiot and she decided to plead guilty so he really wasn't required.'

'I see. But in your opinion Fran was innocent.'

'I don't see why you're pursuing this line, Kate. All these years Fran has been convinced that she did kill Ben, now you come along and tell her the opposite. She needs peace and quiet.'

'She has never said that she actually remembered doing it.'

'It's not something you'd want to remember, is it?' he said sharply.

I paused for thought. 'Do you think it possible someone else killed Ben?'

He shook his head.

'So you think Fran, a woman you are fond of, was capable of killing her own son?'

'Assuredly,' he said. 'I think she killed Ben. And I think you should leave her alone. She'd accepted her guilt, then she met you and it has disturbed her.'

'How can you be so sure?' I asked, unwilling to give up on my conviction that someone else could be responsible.

'Ben's crying annoyed her. She told me once that she felt like killing him.'

CHAPTER TWENTY-TWO

Initially I was shocked at his revelation, but then I remembered how often my mother wanted to kill me. It was one of those meaningless phrases that mothers use, and a crying baby can be very wearing. Perhaps Fran's disclosure was just her being honest rather than homicidal. I wanted him to tell me more but at that moment a plaintive cry from upstairs startled me. The sound, although distant, seemed to echo around the kitchen.

'Malcolm . . . Malcolm, please . . . please.'

'What does she want?' I asked.

'Don't worry about it,' he said with a resigned shrug. 'That's how she is. She isn't able to cope on her own.'

I decided it was time to go. I felt deeply sorry for Malcolm and his wife. They were both isolated in their own misery and however he'd managed to spend time with Fran he still undoubtedly needed a break.

Outside in the street it was still raining but the rain felt fresh and clean and I had to admit I was glad to escape Malcolm's gloomy house and his gloomy life. As far as Fran was concerned I needed to think. I began walking, trying to decide if seeing Fran now would help or hinder my decision. I needed to talk to both Hubert and Alex to hear their views because at the moment I realized I was allowing my emotions to get in the way. I *wanted* her to be innocent.

After walking in the rain for some minutes I was soaked so I managed to hail a taxi and arrived at the Ivy Court Hotel with a sense of relief that a hot bath and a change of clothes was in sight.

Everything about the Ivy Court Hotel reminded me of now-defunct nurses' homes. It was four storeys high and inside had a clean but old-fashioned and jaded appearance. The reception area was manned by an elderly lady with a stern expression and a maroon complexion that matched the threadbare carpet.

'Hello, dear,' she said with a smile. 'I'm Miss Yates, the owner. You do know this is a ladies-only establishment?' I nodded. 'That's good,' she said. 'All our staff are female and I'm afraid there is no lift and no porters.'

I didn't need a porter for my overnight bag. As I signed in she said, 'If you want to be out late please tell me what time you'll be in, then I can arrange to open the door.'

'I don't plan on going out.'

'Good. We don't have a bar or room service but I can always arrange sandwiches for you.'

She directed me to room twelve, which was on the top floor and the room was just as I imagined it: fifty years behind the times. There was even an old gas fire, the type you could make toast on. There was a notice on it saying 'No gas. Please do not attempt to light.' There was an electric kettle and a complimentary tray with ex-NHS blue cups and a tea pot. For some reason there was no television, and although there was a sink in my room I soon found out that the bathroom was shared between two rooms. The floorboards creaked and there was a counterpane on the bed so thin it verged on transparency but the bed itself looked inviting enough with feather pillows and a thick mattress.

I tried it out and it felt as comfortable as it looked. So comfortable that I fell fast asleep but was woken with a start when my mobile rang. It was Hubert.

I felt groggy from sleep but managed to tell him what Malcolm had told me.

'He's a solicitor and her friend so he should know what he's talking about. I think he's right. Leave well alone,' was Hubert's response.

Being a bit obstinate and contrary I knew that whatever he said I'd do just the opposite.

'Your trouble, Kate, is that you always want a happy ending.'

'What's wrong with aiming high?'

'Nothing, but you could make things worse.'

'Fran has lived with the belief she killed her son for six years,' I said. 'What could be worse than that?'

Hubert cleared his throat. 'All right, know-it-all. What if you managed to find out that it was possible for someone else to have done it? Where the hell do you go from there?'

'I'm sure the police would help me then.'

'Don't bank on it. A guilty plea is a closed case.'

'If I got some new evidence they'd have to reopen it, wouldn't they?'

'Ask Simon, he'd know.'

'I'll do that.'

'Try being rational,' he said. 'You can't solve every problem.'

'I'll have a damn good try.'

We chatted for a while about Jasper, and Hubert's staff problems, but I was keen to ring Alex so I told him I had a bath running. 'How's the accommodation?' asked Hubert.

'Very safe,' I said, 'and cheap, as there's no bar.'

'Good. Take care.'

Hubert, bless him, was always concerned for my safety but if I was working on a case I didn't have time to be introspective and depressed. He should be grateful I was working.

I was about to ring Simon when my mobile rang again. It was Fran sounding upset. She'd heard from Malcolm. 'He says I'll be disappointed, that I should stay put for the time being and rest . . .' She broke off. 'I don't need rest. I can't just stay here dusting and polishing. I shall go mad.'

'I'm making progress,' I lied and desperately tried to think of a positive aspect. 'I think I've found your brother-in-law, Giles.'

'My sister?'

'Not yet. But I'll catch Giles tomorrow and I'm sure he will know where she is.'

'He won't tell you. I think he hated me especially as Claudette loved Ben. She's infertile and Giles always wanted to keep us apart.'

'It's a chance I'll take,' I said. 'I can be quite persuasive.'

'If he finds out I'm pregnant he'll . . .'

'What will he do?'

I could hear Fran take a deep breath. 'He certainly won't tell you where my sister is then.'

'I'll see you tomorrow,' I found myself saying. 'Late afternoon.'

'Thank you,' she murmured.

As I put the phone down I realized I'd made a mistake. If I was tearing around London I couldn't waste time Fran-sitting. I glanced at my watch. It was time for dinner at Ivy Court. Please don't let there be semolina on the menu, I silently wished.

The guests had already assembled in the dining room and amongst the sea of silver, grey and salt-and-pepper hair I felt like a teenager. There was some quite raucous laughter and a great deal of talking so I judged it to be a coach load of WI members seeing the sights.

A youngish waitress (anyone under fifty was young here) whispered to me, 'They'll all want you on their table. I'll put you with Veronica and Liz, they're both addicts.'

My mouth opened to object but the waitress was already guiding me towards their table and in unison Veronica and Liz, two well-dressed ladies in their seventies said, 'Hello, Kate. It's so nice to meet you.' They certainly didn't look like addicts. What the hell were they addicted to? Mint imperials?

'I'm sorry,' I said as I sat down. 'What's going on? How do you know my name?'

Liz laughed. 'Miss Yates, of course. She always finds out about new guests.'

'What has she found out?'

'Well, your name is Kate Kinsella,' said Veronica cheerfully. 'You're an ex-nurse and now you're a PI and the two of us are really excited to meet you because we love crime in all its forms.'

'Don't exaggerate, dear,' said Liz. 'We only like reading about it.'

There was no escape. Liz and Veronica were ex-nurses and permanent residents of Ivy Court. We perused the menu, which offered only two choices per course. Melon or soup, beef casserole or roast pork, followed by rice pudding or apple pie with cream. The food was hot and tasty and I began to relax even without the comforting embrace of a glass or two of wine. By the time we reached dessert I'd discussed some of the highlights and lowlights of my investigative career.

'What are you working on now, dear?' asked Liz as she poured coffee from a tray that the waitress had left us.

'I can't discuss it,' I said. 'It's unresolved and rather sad.'

'Do you fancy a drop of brandy in your coffee, dear?' said Liz discreetly showing me a bottle of what appeared to be cough linctus that she'd hidden in her handbag. 'Miss Yates is totally opposed to alcohol so we have to hide it. If we were to be caught we'd simply say the brandy was only used when we were at death's door.'

Veronica laughed and I nodded and watched as she made sure the waitress had her back turned to us and then added a double shot to my coffee cup. Liz had her own supply and after our second pot of coffee and more French 'sugar' we became three very jolly single women. Murder was still their favourite topic of conversation and soon I found myself loose-tongued and talking about infanticide.

'Of course,' said Liz confidently, 'when I worked as a health visitor I saw a big increase in stepfathers and what I called vagrant boyfriends. You know, the type that move in with a single mum because they have nowhere else to go.'

'You're prejudiced,' snapped Veronica. 'Just because you had one or two nasty cases.'

'One child was murdered, that's more than nasty,' said Liz angrily. 'I told Social Services and their GP that he was a man who couldn't tolerate a male child of another man. It's like animals, isn't it? The gene pool has to be pure. Kill the offspring that isn't yours.'

The conversation had darkened and Veronica began drinking the brandy neat from her cough syrup bottle. Liz carried on, 'It's sexual jealousy that causes many killings.'

'Money is more of a motive in the novels I read,' said Veronica.

'Don't you see, V, that money is sex. Its power fuels testosterone. Did you know that if a man who once had money sinks into poverty it's just as if his balls have been crushed?'

'You listen to too much Radio Four, dear,' said Veronica, 'and read the *Guardian*. That's a very unhealthy combination.'

Liz raised her finely pencilled eyebrows. 'You only have to read about the Wall Street crash,' she said, 'to note how many men took the big leap. They knew exactly what poverty would do to their testicles.'

I sat back feeling full and euphoric. I was having the best evening I'd had in a long time. We were about to decamp to the sitting room when my mobile rang. I excused myself to take the call in reception. It was Fran in a panic.

'Come quickly, Kate. There's someone prowling around outside . . . please hurry . . . I'm so scared.'

CHAPTER TWENTY-THREE

Although I urged Fran to calm down in a soothing tone I did wonder why she was ringing me.

'Have you called the police?'

'Of course I have. The operator told me they would come but at the moment they are very busy. I've even rung Malcolm but there was no answer. Please . . . I can't stay here alone.'

'I'm on my way,' I said, 'but it could take me three hours to get to you. In the meantime keep ringing the police if you hear anything outside. Find a weapon and just stay put.'

I made it sound easy but she was obviously scared to death. Prison may have been traumatic and depressing but she'd never been alone there. Now she was pregnant and someone was prowling about outside her isolated cottage. I just hoped she didn't make a bolt for it.

I ran upstairs and threw my belongings in my overnight bag and rushed downstairs to the sitting room to make my breathless apologies to Veronica and Liz. I didn't explain but I did say I would back as soon as I could. 'Good luck, dear. Go get him!' she said as if rousing hounds to the hunt.

Once I'd retrieved my car from near Southgate tube station and found it to be still intact with a full set of wheels

I drove as fast as I dared towards Woburn. I'd phoned Simon on the way. My question to him was: who apart from Malcolm would know where Oak Leaf Cottage was?

'You could have been followed,' he said. 'From Peace Haven to Longborough and then to Woburn.' Surely I'd have noticed? The line was poor but he did manage to tell me that Peace Haven had reopened and that its closure had been an over-reaction. The two men in the 4x4 were gang masters operating illegal asylum seekers working on local farms. They'd both been arrested. We got cut off abruptly, but the last words I heard him say were, 'It might be best if . . .'

By the time I arrived at the Rumbold Estate it was just after ten p.m. The cottage was in darkness. I didn't park the car, I abandoned it, and as I ran towards the door I noticed my footfalls sounded on gravel. New gravel. I banged and called several times before Fran opened the door. Her face was pale, her hair mussed as if she'd been running her hands through it and she smelt strongly of brandy. She pulled me into the dark living room.

'He's still out there,' she whispered. 'I heard him a few minutes ago.'

'First let's put the lights on. Then you can pour me one.'

She flicked on the lights and poured me a large measure from a three-quarter filled bottle. 'I ordered the brandy on the phone,' she explained, sounding ashamed of herself. 'I don't like it but I thought I should have some in for Malcolm. When this happened I couldn't stop myself. I needed — really needed — a drink.'

'How did you pay for it?' I asked.

'I didn't. The local shopkeeper has opened an account for me. He says any tenants on the estate can have an account.'

'How civilized,' I said. 'The police haven't appeared then?'

She shook her head. 'I rang the operator again but she told me the same thing. They were too busy.'

I took off my jacket and sipped the brandy. Hot and fiery, it reminded me I'd already been drinking at the Ivy Court Hotel. Suddenly I hoped the police didn't turn up.

Fran was as jumpy as a pan of popcorn and I had to tell her twice to sit down.

'I just can't relax,' she said. 'I'm so jittery.'

'Did you see anyone or just hear footsteps?'

'I thought I saw a shadow then I heard footsteps on the gravel.'

'Whose idea was the gravel?'

'Mine,' she said. 'I got that on account too.'

I stared at her until she grew uncomfortable.

'Why are you staring at me?' she asked.

'You think you know who's out there, don't you?'

'Of course not. It could be anyone.'

'I don't think it could be anyone,' I said. 'You think it's Neil, don't you?'

She looked away and I knew it was true.

I decided to have a good look around the grounds. There was no torch in the cottage but I had one in my car. I told Fran to shut the door behind me and when that was closed there was enough light to see the gravel. Armed with only my large torch I began looking around the front of the cottage. I looked towards the trees and wondered if that was where the intruder had lurked or was still lurking. Where the gravel ended was muddy grass but there was no sign of footprints. As I rounded the cottage at the back the stream of light from my torch caught a retreating fox. Was that Fran's intruder? Feeling less scared now I approached the back door and the two paving stones that were Fran's only suggestion of a patio. I scanned my torch around, lighthouse fashion, but there was nothing but the odd daffodil and the rustle of leaves. Just as I decided I was wasting my time I checked the back door and windows were secure and was about to turn away when I noticed a mark on the kitchen window. As if someone had pressed their face to look in. I checked the paving stones and there, written in mud, was a fraction of a shoe print — more of a toe print really. Someone had stood or started to stand on the slabs and then turned away.

'Did you find anything?' asked Fran eagerly on my return.

'I saw the backside of a fox, but no sign of human life.'

I took my jacket off and sat down. 'Have you been outside the kitchen this evening?'

She shook her head. 'Why?'

'I think there's a partial footprint out there.'

'I want to look.'

She switched on the kitchen lights and with the extra light of the torch we could see quite clearly its shape. 'But . . .' said Fran, her eyes wide with surprise. 'Surely that's the toe of a woman's shoe.'

'I think it is. The police could make a cast of that.'

I glanced at Fran. Her worried frown now seemed permanent and an air of defeat was noticeable in her body language. I think she wanted to cry but tears can be like rain — unpredictable.

We sat down and drank a little more brandy. I noticed that although Fran was looking tired there was certainly no sign of aggression, no sign that she was losing control. The mystery woman's identity would have to remain a mystery because I felt exhausted. I suggested that Fran thought of the baby and had no more brandy. She then went to bed and I lay down on the sofa. I wasn't offering to be on guard because I knew I couldn't stay awake but at least I'd be dressed and ready for action if necessary.

Sleep didn't come that easily. My mind was full of questions. Had a woman killed Ben? What could she now want with Fran? It didn't make any sense. Nor did the fact that this mystery woman knew where Fran was hiding. Just before sleep finally overtook me I wondered if maybe some female journalist had followed us from the prison. Perhaps she was merely after an exclusive photo of the 'Baby Killer' in her secret hideaway.

I was in a deep sleep when I later heard footsteps on the gravel. I was instantly on high alert, heavy torch at the ready, and my heart was hammering in my chest.

CHAPTER TWENTY-FOUR

The banging on the door was followed by shouts of 'It's the police.' I was already on my feet, my heart rate was beginning to slow and I took a deep breath before opening the door. Behind the two cops in the doorway the rain was beating down and taking the footprint evidence with it.

Fran appeared just then and told the two male officers what she'd seen and heard.

'We don't usually have any trouble around here,' said the older of the two.

'Probably just a burglar,' said the other, as if a burglar was as harmless as a field mouse.

We told them about the footprint, not mentioning its size, but they shrugged. 'Pity it's raining,' said the senior constable who wore rimless glasses and whose uniform hardly buttoned over his paunch. 'Any chance of a cuppa?'

Fran left the room to make tea and after a minute or so I joined her. 'I can't stay here on my own,' she said. 'I can't settle to anything — it's too isolated here.'

'What about going back to Peace Haven?'

'I'll think about it.'

We drank tea with the two police officers and they angled to find out what exactly we were doing at Oak Leaf

Cottage. Fran was quick to reply. 'I'm recuperating after an illness.'

I noticed the older man looking at Fran quizzically and she was quick to respond.

'I'm not feeling too well,' she said. 'I'm going back to bed. Thank you for coming.'

I breathed a sigh of relief when they'd gone. The police arriving after an event is about as useful as being soaked through and then being offered an umbrella when the rain has stopped.

Fran came downstairs again when she heard their car drive away. She sat on the sofa clutching her knees and staring at the floor.

'Why?' I asked her. 'Why did you suspect Neil was stalking about outside?'

It took her some time to answer, then in a slow, measured way she looked at me and said, 'Neil was devoted to Ben. He'd always wanted boys. Fiona was a bit of a disappointment to him. At first he didn't blame me but very soon he too was totally convinced I'd killed our son. He became very bitter and very angry. In one fell swoop he'd lost both his wife — the breadwinner — and his beloved son. After I was arrested he was allowed to see me. Without any hint of emotion he said, in the most matter-of-fact way, that when I was released he'd kill me.'

'Why didn't you tell me this before?'

She shrugged. 'What would be the point? He would be just one amongst a few other deranged souls who would like to see me dead.'

'Among them a woman, unless our intruder was a journalist,' I said.

'I really have to leave here now, don't I?'

'Yes. I'll drive you back to Peace Haven.'

'No. I'll go there by taxi. Malcolm gave me some emergency money. Driving me to Wales is just a waste of your time. I want you to find me innocent and find Fiona. I know that will take time.'

'I will do my best, Fran,' I said. 'But six years is a long time and I may not be successful.'

She smiled sadly. 'If you don't succeed I'll ask to go on the regular witness protection programme — change my name, perhaps train for another career . . .' She broke off, her eyes bright, her voice husky.

'Come on,' I said, trying to jolly her along. 'You go and pack. I'll cook breakfast, tidy up and order a cab. You can be off by seven a.m.'

'OK,' she said miserably. Then she added, 'I've failed. I thought I could hack being alone in this cottage. It seems for someone who was once successful I've lost my life force.'

'Don't think like that,' I said, putting an arm around her. 'Look to the future. It can't get any worse than the recent past.'

My words seemed facile but sometimes the old clichés hold simple truths and a bit of comfort. She didn't look comforted but she went upstairs to pack and I began phoning around for a taxi to take her to Wales. Five phone calls later I'd managed to find a taxi driver willing to take her at the cost of £150. For that she could have flown to Spain but the price was agreed and he would arrive at seven thirty a.m.

* * *

Later that day, back in London with my car parked almost in the same place in Southgate, I went first to the Ivy Court Hotel, saw Miss Yates and booked my room for a further three nights. She was most understanding. 'It goes with the territory,' she said. 'Supper's at six thirty but if you're late we won't see you starve.'

My next trip on the underground was back to the scene of the crime. This time I planned to speak to the neighbours on either side. The house to the left looked a little shabby but still majestic. The woman who answered the door wearing an apron and holding a can of furniture polish was probably the cleaner but I couldn't be sure. 'Mrs Carter-Jones?' I queried.

She shook her head. 'I'm the cleaner, Gloria.'

'Have you been working here some years?' I asked. She looked about fifty, her hair was dyed a serious black and scraped back to form a spiky pony tail.

'Yeah. About ten,' she said. 'What do you want?'

I came straight to the point. 'I'm a private investigator dealing with the death of Benjamin Rowley.'

She looked me up and down. 'You're not from the newspapers then?'

I assured her that I wasn't and she directed me downstairs to a basement kitchen very similar to how I imagined the Rowleys' might have looked.

'It's time for my tea break,' she said. 'Fancy one?'

I nodded and she indicated where I should sit at the glass-topped table. Gloria was a big woman but her movements were quick and I guessed her brain was equally quick.

'You've come to the right place,' she said. 'I used to clean next door as well. Two days at this place and three next door.'

'Were you questioned by the police at the time?'

'Oh, yeah. They asked me all sorts of questions. Did I often hear them rowing, that sort of thing.'

'Did you?'

'Couldn't very well, could I? Mrs Rowley was nearly always at work. And in my line of work it pays to be deaf and blind. No one wants to employ a blabbermouth, do they?'

'I hadn't thought of it like that.'

'No, neither had the police. So I acted thick as a plank and it was like we were from the same tree,' she said. 'Get it?'

'Got it.'

Gloria added another sugar to her tea and stirred it with quiet intensity. 'I wasn't there when it happened but poor little Fiona was so shocked she couldn't speak. If she'd been my granddaughter I'd have taken her away from the house but his lordship insisted she needed normality and her nanny Erin.'

'You didn't like Neil Rowley much then?'

'Do you want it put bluntly, love?'

I nodded.

'He was an arrogant, lazy little shit.'

'And Fran?'

Gloria smiled. 'She was a lovely woman. I saw more of her just after Ben was born and she was a diamond of a mum.'

'So you were surprised when Mrs Rowley pleaded guilty?'

'Surprised! I was bloody flabbergasted. She wasn't in her right mind when she admitted it. I still don't believe she had it in her.'

'What did you think about Erin?'

'I heard her yelling at the kids a few times. She was a strange girl. Went to church and talked about Mary and the angels quite a bit. But she wasn't as pure as the driven snow.'

'You mean she had lots of boyfriends?'

'Lots of girlfriends more like, if you know what I mean. I reckon that's why Mr Rowley always seemed fascinated by her. He painted her quite a few times 'cause she was a pretty girl.'

'Were they nude paintings?'

'No. His other women friends he painted in the nude.' She paused thoughtfully. 'I don't think Mrs Rowley knew what he was doing in that attic. It had a pull-down ladder, quite safe but as far as I know she never ventured up there. I had to give the place a bit of clean. Not that I managed it every week.'

'Tell me about the paintings.'

'I'm no judge but they weren't very good. His women friends didn't look real, they looked like dolls, but the paintings of Erin were different.'

'In what way?'

'They looked like her but she was always the Madonna or something religious. A bit odd 'cause he told me in didn't believe in religion.'

'Do you think he was in love with Erin?'

'I dunno but he sort of followed her around all the time.'

Gloria poured more tea and began wiping surfaces. 'I know you're busy,' I said, 'but I think someone else killed Ben and that Fran Rowley was the fall guy. The police said there was no sign of a forced entry so if no one else was in the house it must have been Fran.'

'Or Fiona,' muttered Gloria.

CHAPTER TWENTY-FIVE

I stared at Gloria. 'Don't look at me like that,' she said. 'These things 'appen. Some kids get jealous. Who knows what goes on in their minds? Fiona was a nice kid but she missed her mum. Sometimes when I was working and Erin was busy with Ben she'd follow me around with a duster. Once she asked if she could come home with me. Poor little mite.'

Gloria wasn't a child psychologist but I guessed her life experiences were as valid as any amount of regurgitated theories.

'How did Fiona get on with her dad?' I asked.

Gloria thought for a moment. 'Not bad considering he was always skiving off to paint. I mean, painting pictures isn't a proper job, is it?'

'He did sell a few paintings I believe.'

'I heard he'd sold a couple,' she said, 'but he'd bought that car with the money.'

Gloria stood up, took a J cloth from a drawer, moistened it with washing-up liquid and began cleaning the front of the fridge.

'Tell me about the Rowleys' arrangements with the back gate and the back door,' I said.

She paused for a moment with her back to me then carried on cleaning. 'What do mean — arrangements?'

'Was the back gate always locked, and the back door?'

'The back door was never locked in the day, I know that,' said Gloria. 'But I don't know what happened at night.'

'What about the back gate?'

'I always came in that way and it was always unlocked. That back gate was a bugger to lock anyway. There was something wrong with the lock.'

'Would Erin have always locked it?'

Gloria stopped dabbing with her cloth and sat down. 'Erin was OK with the kids but she had a memory like a sieve. Once when it was raining she took the back door key out so Fiona couldn't go out in the garden and she couldn't remember where she'd put it.'

'Was the lock changed?'

Gloria shook her head. 'No, they used the spare key.'

'No one seemed very security-conscious,' I commented.

'I reckon they thought because it was a posh area they shouldn't have to worry. There was a burglar alarm but it kept going off for no reason so they stopped using it.'

Gloria's hands kept touching her cleaning cloth and I sensed I was outstaying my welcome.

'Just one more question,' I said. 'Then I'll leave you in peace.'

'Fire away.'

'How did Fiona get on at school?'

'Fine. She was very bright. She was reading quite well at four.'

'Private school?'

'Of course. The prep school just round the corner on the left. It's called Livingstone-Lovell. It's very small, only about thirty kids, so they get the attention. That's what you pay for, isn't it?'

I agreed that it was, thanked her and I was at the front door when I asked a question I didn't think she could answer but thought it was worth a try.

'I suppose you haven't any idea where Neil may have taken Fiona?'

Gloria looked at me closely. 'You really are trying to help Mrs Rowley, aren't you?'

'Yes. I am,' I said firmly.

'It was a bad time afterwards. He was in a real state; all bitter and twisted. He said no one was to contact his wife and he told Fiona her mother had gone to hospital and was so ill that she wouldn't get better. Fiona begged to see her mother but he always made some excuse.'

'Where did they go, Gloria?'

'One day I overheard him on the phone and I heard him mention Norfolk. I knew Ben had been buried in Norfolk because I went to the funeral but one day I caught sight of an estate agent's details. It was for a cottage in Cromer called Angel View.'

'Did he know you'd found out?'

She shook her head and smiled. 'He thought I was deaf, dumb, daft and blind. Terrible snob, he was. He could be there. I don't know the exact address but can't be many cottages called Angel View. It looked like it was overlooking the sea and Fiona loved the sea just like her mum.'

'Gloria, you've been the most helpful person I've met. Thanks a million.'

'You're welcome, love, my pleasure. I wish you luck — will you let me know?'

I promised her I would and walked into the sunshine that now gave the white fronts of the Holland Park houses a gilding of light that enhanced everything from potted pines and plants to the smart brass knockers and the odd stained-glass window. My heart sang too and although I tried to temper my optimism it didn't stop me entering a very up-market coffee house where I sat amongst smart older women, sipped my expensive coffee and ate a Danish pastry that cost what in Longborough would have paid for lunch.

From there it was a short walk to Livingstone-Lovell Preparatory school. The building itself was indistinguishable from other houses but for the sign which told me it was for children between 2.5 and 11 years. The headmistress was a Miss Paula Ford: BA (Hons), MA.

Once inside the school I was struck by the atmosphere of quiet homeliness. The elderly school secretary who'd opened the door to me spoke in a voice a mere decibel or so above a whisper. I was taken via the hallway, which was decorated with children's paintings, past closed doors to the head's office which wasn't much bigger than a pantry and, it seemed, had a permanently open door.

Paula Ford was in her forties, slim and attractive, wearing a grey skirt, white blouse, high heels and immaculate make-up. Her dark hair was cut in a fashionable choppy style and her air of total confidence managed to make me feel ill at ease. She didn't seem at all surprised that I'd come to talk about Fiona, although I didn't tell her I was a PI. I told her I was a writer researching the effects of sibling loss and asked if she remembered Fiona Rowley. We sat down, the door still open, and she gave me her full attention.

'I certainly do,' she said. 'What a tragedy. What do you want to know?'

I was a little surprised at how easily she had accepted my mock persona. I half expected her to mention client confidentiality but after six years and with so much publicity maybe it didn't apply.

'Could you tell me what sort of child she was, prior to her mother's death?'

Paula Ford smiled. 'Very bright, sociable but a little needy, according to her class teacher. I remember her very well. I was new here and she was sent to my office twice in my first week.'

'What for?'

'Talking in class. Some schools allow far more noise than we do but we have established here a very peaceful, calm environment.'

'What did you say to her?'

'I told her that if she needed to talk she should ask to leave the classroom so that she could come and talk to me.'

'Did she ever do that?'

'Once or twice.'

'Do you mind if I ask what she talked about?'

'Not at all. She told me she didn't see her mummy very much and it seems she tried to stay awake at night so that she could see her mother when she came home from work. It seems she felt almost guilty that she couldn't manage to do that.'

'Would you say she was a happy child?'

There was a short pause before Miss Ford said, 'Not as carefree as some children. A little precocious perhaps but generally she seemed happy.'

'Did she ever mention Benjamin?'

'Once. She said it was better now that Benjamin was walking because she could hold his hand and teach him things.'

'Did she return to school after her brother's death?'

'Yes. Almost immediately, but sadly she was a changed child. She worked well but hardly spoke. She refused to have anything to do with her best friend Zoe, and after about a year they moved away.'

'Do you know where they went?'

'To the seaside, I think.'

'An increase in violent behaviour after a sibling's death has been reported in some research papers,' I said, sounding, I thought, very professional. 'Did you notice any volatile behaviour in Fiona?'

'None at all. Fiona had a gentle nature and afterwards I think she was depressed. I did talk to her father and suggested she saw their GP but I'm sorry to say Mr Rowley refused. He thought a change of scene was all she needed.'

I noted a slight change of tone now that Neil had been mentioned.

'You didn't approve?'

'I didn't. I thought she needed some area of consistency in her life. This school would have provided that.'

'Did she ever mention her mother?'

'Never.' She paused, deep in thought. 'For a five-year-old she was quite a good little artist but after the tragedy she only produced only one sort of painting. White flowers with long stamens. When I asked them what they were she said, "Lilies". I don't know if she thought there was a funeral connection or if she just liked them. So I asked her. She said, "I dream about them." I presumed then her mother liked them.'

'How odd,' I murmured.

'I thought so too,' said Paula. 'I mentioned the lilies to Mr Rowley and he seemed to think it was the artist in her. He said rather archly that his wife hadn't been particularly fond of lilies.'

I was about to thank her and leave when she said, 'Mr Rowley did ask us to be aware that he had told Fiona her mother was dead. I did tell him I didn't approve of telling her lies but he was most insistent.' She paused and looked a little uncomfortable. 'Children can be very aware and of course the older children read newspapers or saw the television news so it was impossible to maintain such a lie and I believe some taunting went on. Poor Fiona must have been very confused.'

'That was probably why she was taken away from the school.'

'Yes, and I believe her father had plans to send her to boarding school as soon as possible.'

'Not at five years old, surely?'

'She was nearly six when she left but from his tone it seemed he planned to send her at quite a young age.'

That was something Gloria hadn't overheard but in the quest to find Fiona it could be a breakthrough.

CHAPTER TWENTY-SIX

An hour and a half later, with grey skies above, I stood outside the Kensington home of one of 'Neil's Nudies' as I was now calling them. I checked names and addresses in my notes and was grateful that both women lived within walking distance. There was no answer from my repeated knocking at the home of Anita Hanwell. I decided to wait for a while and it was then that I really missed my car. At least sucking mints and listening to the radio I wouldn't look as if I were loitering with intent. After a few minutes of standing still and feeling as conspicuous as a nun at a rave I began walking slowly away up the street passing a traffic warden and a woman walking a proud black poodle. Then I turned around and walked slowly back. After a few tedious minutes I decided I was wasting my time. Just as I began walking away a woman jogger came into view. Her long blonde hair was swept back with a red sweat band and her breasts remained fairly steady beneath a black track suit top. As she came alongside me I could see she was older than I'd thought and as she stopped outside of her Georgian pile I felt a sense of triumph at meeting the first of 'Neil's Nudies'.

'I don't see why I should speak to you,' she said breathlessly after I'd introduced myself. There were four steps up to her house she was on the fourth and looking down on me. 'What on earth can I tell you? I haven't see Neil in years.'

I shrugged. 'Fine,' I said. 'I'll go to your husband's office. I'm sure he'll talk to me.'

Her enhanced lips mouthed a swear word, she turned away and took her keys from the pocket of her gold striped jogging bottoms. I also turned away, disappointed. She opened the door, 'Come on in,' she called. 'I haven't got all day.'

From her giant fridge in a modern chrome and steel kitchen she selected a bottle of white wine already opened and poured me a glass. When I look surprised she said, 'Any time is good for a glass of wine. If you don't want it I'll drink it.'

I wasn't driving and, being easily led, I began sipping. For Anita it was more like knocking it back. She finished the glass as if it were water. 'I was thirsty as hell,' she said as she refilled her glass. We sat down on chrome bar stools at the breakfast bar and she stared at me. 'You don't jog, do you?' It wasn't a question. 'I bet you don't diet either.'

She didn't wait for my reply. 'Anyway, what do you want to know about Neil and why?'

'I think Fran may be innocent of killing her son,' I said bluntly. 'I wondered if you had an address for him.'

Strangely she showed no surprise. 'Neil wouldn't be able to help you and I don't know where he is anyway.'

'I've been told you had a relationship with Neil.'

'I don't know who told you that and I don't bloody care. I was a friend of Neil's, that's all.'

'Were you a friend of Fran's too?'

She shook her head. 'I had nothing in common with Fran. She despised me although she tried not to show it. After all, what have I achieved in life? I married a rich man. I'm a size ten, I've been breast-enhanced, face-lifted, Botoxed and I allowed some maniac to suck out fat from my thighs. I'm forty years old; my husband is fifty-five, fat and boring. End of story.'

'Tell me about Fran,' I said.

Silently Anita took a large gulp of wine, stood up, walked to the fridge and, standing on tip toes, retrieved a silver ash tray, packet of cigarettes and a lighter from the top of the fridge. Then she sat down again, offered me a cigarette which I declined, lit hers and inhaled deeply. 'I've been trying to give up for five years,' she said. 'Fran, of course, had no bad habits. The most you could say about her was that she was always tired.'

'You don't sound as if you had much sympathy for her.'

'I don't do sympathy. For an intelligent woman she could be incredibly stupid.'

'In what way?'

'She slaved away while Neil enjoyed non-strenuous attempts at being an artist.'

'I believe your husband paid a large amount for one of his paintings.'

She smiled, showing her expensive dentistry which she'd forgotten to mention. 'I insisted that I couldn't live without the painting. Actually it was crap. I didn't look real but then most of me isn't, so in that why I suppose it was . . . honest.'

'Did Neil need the money?'

'No, I wanted to carry on shagging him.' I raised an eyebrow. 'I'm being honest,' she said as she blew smoke above my head. 'We simply used each other. He despised me as I despised Fran but that didn't stop us having great sex.'

'So you weren't in love with him?'

'Of course not,' she snapped. 'He had lots of superficial charm, good looks and a great body but I couldn't respect a man who treated his wife so badly.'

'In what way did he treat her badly? Surely Fran was a "have it all woman" — husband, two children, a well-paid job, nanny, car, great house. What more could she want?'

Anita stubbed out her cigarette and stared at me momentarily. 'You don't know her very well, do you?'

'What do you mean?'

'I mean Fran's life, notwithstanding the assets as you listed them, wasn't a happy one. Sometimes I thought she worked such long hours to escape from him.'

'Why should she need to escape from him?'

'He was an insecure man, not a brilliant accountant and a piss-poor artist. Fran was either too tired or too preoccupied to have sex with him and he had a violent temper.'

'You're saying he hit her?'

'She didn't admit it. She used every excuse under the sun if she had a bruise.'

I was truly surprised and shocked. 'Why didn't this come out in court?'

Anita shrugged. 'I suppose because by then she knew she would go to prison and she couldn't run the risk of Fiona losing both her father and her mother.'

I'd harboured a vague hope that one day Fran and Neil might be reconciled but now a different scenario was beginning to emerge. He didn't seem the sort of man who would allow Fran any access to Fiona at all. If he thought his only child might be taken from him Fran herself might be in danger. I finished my wine and was about to go before my spirits plummeted further when Anita poured herself the last of the wine.

'I'll tell you this about Neil,' she said. 'He was a passionate man, weak and vain, but he loved Fran very much and here's the twist: when he was having sex with me he'd murmur her name.'

As I walked away from the house I really didn't feel I wanted to see anyone else that day. I needed to think. I rang Hubert as I was walking along.

'How's it going?' he asked cheerfully.

'It's complicated,' I said. 'I don't know what to think any more. I'm pretty sure I know where Neil is living but Fiona could be at a boarding school anywhere in the country.'

'Where's Fran?'

'She's gone back to Peace Haven.'

'She'll be safe there.'

'I just don't know what to do now, Hubert. I can talk to people that knew the Rowleys and keep getting different perspectives but that doesn't help me find the murderer.'

'Could be you're looking for someone who doesn't exist,' he said softly.

CHAPTER TWENTY-SEVEN

I knew that Hubert could be right and although I wasn't willing to give up yet, at that moment I felt despondent. It was beginning to look overcast and I knew rain couldn't be far away. Traffic was heavy and the phone line so crackly that I had to strain to hear Hubert's quiet voice.

'Where are you?' he asked.

'Kensington, but I don't know where to go next.'

'If I were you I'd have a pub lunch. You don't function when you're hungry.'

'And then what?'

'I think you should find Fran's sister; after all no one would know her better.'

'You could be right on both counts — food and sister — but . . .'

'No buts, just get on with it. Jasper's missing you.'

Taking heed of Hubert's advice I realized I probably did need to eat. The wine on an empty stomach hadn't been a good idea. I spotted several taxis but they were taken and I was still looking for one when the heavens opened. I hadn't bought an umbrella, there was nowhere to shelter and within minutes I was soaked through. Now I was in no state for a pub lunch and I started walking briskly towards Kensington

High Street hoping that there was a taxi haven. My saviour came in the form of an elderly bald man with a strangely heavy moustache and a strong cockney accent. He delivered me to the Ivy Court Hotel and whilst he drove he gave me health advice. 'If you want to avoid pneumonia, sweetheart, you need a hot bath, two aspirins and two double whiskies. It works for me every time.'

'I'll do that,' I said, which seemed to satisfy him.

Miss Yates was sitting in reception and I realized I'd never actually seen her standing up. She gave me the same advice as the taxi driver, minus the whisky. 'I'll get a selection of sandwiches sent up in about twenty minutes,' she said. 'Have you had any luck?' She obviously knew I was no mere tourist but it was still a little disconcerting that so many people were taking an interest. Failure would be humiliating, I told myself, think positively.

I felt positive after a hot bath and even more positive after a large plate of sandwiches. So positive did I feel that I fell asleep in a comfy glow of boosted confidence. I slept for four hours and woke feeling groggy and less than in touch with my cognitive abilities, dimmed I thought from not having watched *Countdown* for some time.

By seven p.m. I was seated in the dining room at a table for two and was relieved to find I had no companion. There were no familiar faces and I was more than happy to eat alone whilst listening to four middle-aged women talking about the men in their lives from the table beside me.

'Husbands always go the same way,' said the loudest of the group. 'They get to forty-five or so and as their testosterone fails their thoughts turn from passion between the sheets to gardening.'

'That's a sweeping generalization, Myra,' said the woman next to her. 'Some men want to keep the flame of passion alive, just with someone else.'

'You should know,' retorted Myra. 'You are on your third husband.'

'That's true but not one of them has turned to gardening.'

A different voice said, 'Men do get fixated, obsessed. My husband pursued me for two years before I agreed to go out with him.'

'But you don't regret marrying him, do you?'

There was a short pause before she replied, 'I do regret it. He was never normal. He thought he was protecting me from the world like a security blanket. The trouble is that all a security blanket does in the end is suffocate. And I did feel suffocated.'

'Are you still with him?' asked a new timid voice.

'He killed himself.' That was a real conversation stopper. 'Don't feel sorry for me,' she said. 'I've never been happier.'

Overhearing their chat had been a thought-provoking interlude but I didn't have time to linger. I didn't wait for coffee but ordered a taxi from reception and ten minutes later I was on my way to meet Fran's brother-in-law and hopefully her sister as well.

After paying for the taxi and taking a minute or two to recover from the cost I rang Ian Skipton's door bell. The lights were on but getting a response seemed to take forever. When the door did open it was obvious Ian had been in the shower; his hair was wet and he wore a white towelling bathrobe. Square-faced with a large head and a stocky body, if I could have chosen a name for him it would have been Boris.

'Yes?' he said.

'I'm sorry to bother you,' I began apologetically. 'I'm a PI working on behalf of your sister-in-law, Fran—'

He didn't let me finish. 'I've got nothing to say,' he said, about to close the door on me.

'Could I see your wife?' I asked.

'She's not here,' he snapped. 'If you must know, she's left me.'

'I'm sorry,' I said. 'Do you have her address?'

He stared at me, and then after a long pause he sighed in resignation. 'You'd better come in.'

The house was a womanless tip. Clothes lay strewn on the floor of the living room. The remains of a takeaway meal, several used mugs and tumblers covered the surface of a coffee table. Newspapers lay in random piles and the smell in the room was of palpable neglect — airless and musty. 'I can't find a cleaner and I work long hours,' he said, obviously embarrassed. Then he added, 'Find a place to sit while I get dressed.'

While he was upstairs I had a cursory glance through a small pile of photos that lay on a half-empty bookcase. There were several snaps of Claudette alone wearing bikinis or lounging on sofas and showing off her long legs. I had to admit she was far prettier than her sister. Although less angular in both face and body than Fran it was her eyes that held my attention. They seemed to be staring into the far distance as though there was another place she wanted to be. Maybe I was being fanciful but when I came across one photo of the sisters together at a party Fran looked radiant whereas Claudette had that same expression.

I didn't hear him creep up behind me. 'You could have asked,' he said. 'You'd better sit down.' He cleared an armchair of unopened junk mail and I sat down. He stood over me dressed in jeans and a navy sweatshirt and wearing a frown. 'What's all this about? I thought we'd heard the last of Fran Rowley.'

'I'm hoping that new evidence might be found and . . .'

He didn't let me finish. 'What new evidence, for God's sake? She pleaded guilty. There's no more to be said.'

'I think there is.'

'Who the hell do you think you are? That woman has caused us so much trouble. You have no idea.'

'I won't unless you tell me.'

He needed to think about that and the following silence was long and awkward — the sort of silence that needs strong nerves not to break. Eventually he sat down and said, 'Claudette idolized her sister. Fran was clever, ambitious — everything that Claudette wasn't . . .' He broke off. 'And of course she was fertile. Claudette cannot have children so she focused on Fran's.'

'And you didn't approve?'

'If you must know, I didn't. I thought seeing those kids made Claudette more broody and more dissatisfied. According to my wife Fran had the perfect life.'

'And you didn't think so?'

'Married to that lazy, womanizing, egocentric bastard — I think not.'

'That made you angry?'

'Of course it made me angry,' he snapped. 'I wanted to make my wife happy but I couldn't. She wanted to adopt but I couldn't do that either.'

'Why not?'

He stared at me as if not believing I could be so stupid. 'Because I don't want to see another man's child in my wife's arms.'

'Would it make a difference if that child was male or female?' I asked.

'I've never given it a thought,' he said, frowning. 'I'm going to have a drink. Do you want one?'

I shook my head and he left the room returning seconds later with a bottle of malt whisky and a glass. 'I keep the whisky in the kitchen,' he explained. 'It means I get the exercise walking back and forth. Tonight I'm keeping it to hand.' He poured at least a triple carefully, sat down and took a steady gulp followed by another. 'I've given your last question a brief thought,' he said, 'and I've come to the conclusion that I could cope with a female child.'

He didn't seem the ideal adopter to me, but thankfully that wasn't my problem or his at the moment. Was it possible that he could have killed Benjamin in a jealous or drunken rage? If so he would need access to the house and a pretext for being there. Did he in fact have an alibi for that evening?

'Why did you even ask the question?' he said.

'Because I think it possible that a man could have killed Fran's son.'

'I think you're mad,' he said, 'and greedy, because no doubt Fran is paying you to ask pointless questions. She wants to see her daughter again and she'll go to any lengths to achieve that.'

'Can you give me a reason why Fran shouldn't see her daughter?'

'Of course I can. How can she be trusted with another child?'

'Everyone I've spoken to has said that she was a good, loving mother. Do you think differently?'

He shrugged. 'I don't think a good mother works twelve hours a day and leaves her children in the hands of others.'

'You mean their father and a trained nanny aren't suitable people.'

'I didn't say that.'

'No, but you implied it.'

He drained his whisky glass. 'I think it's time you went.'

'I'd appreciate Claudette's address.'

'She's living in Harpenden in a flat above a bakery. Number twenty-four Lower End Lane.'

I thanked him, stood up and as I moved towards the door I said, 'One last question.'

He nodded and smiled as if in relief that I was going.

'Did you have a key to the Rowleys' house?' I asked.

There was a pause in which an expression of unease momentarily crossed his face.

'No, I've never had one.'

'You're sure?'

'Of course I'm bloody sure.' I was at the front door when he said, 'Claudette had a key. She used to go there quite often.'

CHAPTER TWENTY-EIGHT

In Harpenden the next day the sun shone and I walked along the main street just to enjoy the town's up-market atmosphere. I was a tad worried because Fran hadn't phoned me but I knew the regime at Peace Haven didn't encourage communication with the outside world so I'd have to be patient.

I'd spoken to Hubert and told him that Fran's sister had owned a key to the Rowley property. To his dire warnings I listened and gave him the equivalent response of the married "Yes dear, no dear" which was a resigned "Yeah yeah, OK."

I found the bakery on Lower End Lane, which, as its name suggested, was in the less affluent part of town. The shop itself was tiny and the selection of bread and cakes didn't compare with the two other bakeries in the town but even so I bought two fat jam doughnuts. The flat above the shop had a front door adjacent to the shop and I rang the doorbell several times before I heard footsteps.

Compared to her photos Claudette looked older and thinner. She wore faded jeans and a blue tee shirt that hung loosely on her and her eyes had a haunted expression that reminded me of someone in shock, reinforced when I told her why I'd come.

We climbed the steep stairs to her flat that was small and smelt of yeast and she offered me either a sofa or an armchair. Although it was a small room it was clean and tidy with pot plants as ornaments and with a vase of red roses on a coffee table. She saw me glancing at the roses and said, 'They're from my husband. He wants me back; he's not coping very well.'

We sat down and Claudette raked her hands through her long dark hair in a sort of depressed resignation. 'Has something happened to Fran?' she asked.

'No,' I said. 'She's fine. She's been freed from prison and she's staying in a safe house.'

'I'm glad,' she murmured.

I was surprised at her being so calm. I'd suspected her response would be bitter and vitriolic. 'You didn't visit her in prison,' I said, 'or respond to her letters.'

She looked at me with her melancholy eyes. 'I was heart-broken when Ben died. He was the happiest baby and toddler you could ever meet. I loved Fiona too and I suppose I thought of Ben as the son I'd never have.'

'You saw them a lot?'

There was a pause before she said softly, 'Yes.'

'Was that at the weekends?'

'I'm so tired of the worry,' she murmured.

'What do you mean?'

Claudette looked away. 'I used to go there in the day, most days. Neil was either in the attic painting or he was out so I spent loads of time with the kids.'

'That doesn't sound so bad.'

'Maybe not,' she sighed. 'But I didn't tell Fran and when Fiona could talk it was our little secret.'

'Why not tell Fran?'

'I knew she'd be jealous. Both children seemed to treat me as their mother. Often Fran came home so late they were already in bed. In the two weeks before Ben died I saw Fran once. She was exhausted, preoccupied and drinking too much.'

'What about the nanny Erin in all this?'

'It suited her. She had a girlfriend who worked from home and so in the day she could visit her.'

'I've seen Erin and she didn't tell me any of this.'

'Neither she nor Neil wanted to be seen in a bad light, especially when Fran pleaded guilty.'

'It seems to me,' I said, 'that no one even tried to plead mitigating circumstances on Fran's behalf. She was still in shock at the time of the hearing and unable to speak up for herself, and no one else was prepared to see beyond the "ambitious, hard-drinking career woman" that the newspapers portrayed. You knew her best of all — do you think she could have killed her child?'

Claudette shook her head as her eyes filled with tears. 'I didn't think so but she admitted it. The police didn't bother once she'd confessed — why should they?'

'Has it *ever* crossed your mind in the past six years that someone else could have killed Ben?'

'No. Why should it? Fran was seriously stressed and she knew Neil was cheating on her. So I suppose she had some sort of breakdown.'

'To me she seems remarkably resilient.'

Claudette paused. 'Yes, she was. Fran always persevered no matter what. She was always the responsible, hard-working one. I just wanted an easy life.'

'You sound,' I said, 'as if you care about her.'

'I do. I do care. I've always loved her. She was always there for me.'

'So why not stand by her when she needed you?'

Claudette looked down and said quietly, 'My soon to be ex-husband made it clear: I chose my sister or him. For all this time I chose him and once I'd made that choice and told him he said I was never to go anywhere near the family again.'

'Told him what?' I asked, puzzled.

'Told him that I was addicted to heroin.'

I took a deep breath. This wasn't what I expected. 'He didn't know?'

'I was very good at covering up and . . .' She broke off. 'Erin told me she was friendly with a doctor, a doctor who was giving her methadone prescriptions for her *friend*, which is the only reason she saw him. When I found that out I paid her to get me prescriptions for methadone. I've been clean now for a year.'

'Bully for you,' I said.

'It is an illness,' she said. 'It was the biggest struggle of my life but once I was free of heroin and methadone I saw clearly what he'd done to me. I expect he told you I was the infertile one but he's the one firing blanks. He refused to discuss adoption so I left him.'

I remembered her eyes in the photo — not sad and far-away as I'd thought; she was in fact spaced out.

'Did Neil know any of this?' I asked.

'No. Not at the time. I told him after the funeral. He sacked Erin on the spot and said he never wanted to see me again. He's the type of man who disapproves of the vices and lifestyles of others but the same rules don't apply to him. He's a hypocritical bastard.'

'You haven't seen him or Fiona since?'

She shook her head. 'That poor little mite lost her mother, me and her nanny all within a year.'

'Do you know where he and Fiona are living now?'

'Yes. Getting off the habit and moving here I'm hoping that one day I'll see Fiona again. She's eleven now. She wrote to me from her boarding school. She hates it there, she says she cries a lot and she has no friends. She often has bad dreams.'

'Which school is she at?'

'Danescroft; it's about ten miles from Cromer.'

'Have you got a photo?'

'No, but I can show you one of Fran at the same age. There're very much alike.'

Claudette went into the bedroom to find the photo leaving me with the feeling that although I was making progress I was no nearer finding Ben's killer than I was before.

The photo of Fran and Claudette in their school uniforms at ages eleven and seven showed they were both tall for their ages. Fran had her long dark hair in plaits whereas Claudette's hair was fair and curly and framed her cherubic face. Fran wore a serious expression and I felt sure I would recognize her child amongst several.

'Do you want to see Fran again?' I asked.

'Of course I do. Now I'm clean of drugs and rid of my husband, I just want to start again.'

'Good,' I said. 'Fran is in a safe house at the moment but before I see her again I need to talk to Neil and Fiona.'

'Fiona doesn't remember anything about that night, you know. She had nightmares for weeks.'

'Did she ever say what they were about?' I asked.

'Yes. She told me. She said she saw white flowers and those white flowers meant everyone she knew would die.'

CHAPTER TWENTY-NINE

I checked out of the Ivy Court Hotel the next morning after the rush hour and began my journey to Norfolk. I'd slept badly. It seemed to me now that I'd given Claudette an easy ride. After all, she had been a heroin addict and addicts can be notoriously unreliable. She'd had access to the Rowley home and she'd envied Fran's children. Had envy become pure jealousy and rage? Somehow I doubted that and I trusted my first instinct that Claudette was not the person I was looking for.

Erin the nanny was still a contender; she'd had opportunity and could have killed Ben *before* she left the house, expecting Fran to check on him a little later. But did she have a motive? Perhaps a motive, I thought, for abduction of the child, her lesbian lover being desperate for them to be a 'proper' family. I didn't find that convincing so I concentrated on the questions I wanted to ask Neil and, more importantly, the other person present on the night Ben was killed: Fiona.

As I drove I was aware of how tired I'd become. I stopped three times on the journey towards Cromer and although perked up by coffee the effects didn't last long. I'd now realized that this investigation needed a whole team of people.

As far as I could see no one had had a motive to kill young Benjamin except someone who was mentally deranged or whose balance of mind was momentarily disturbed. Someone who appeared normal, functioned normally, but deep inside that psyche the poison festered like some huge painful abscess that only murder could burst.

I braked sharply at some unexpected traffic lights and decided to find a lay-by and make a few phone calls. I rang Hubert first. 'You sound hungover,' he said.

'I'm not,' I said. 'I'm driving to Cromer and I'm tired.'

'Well, get off the road then.'

'I am off the road. I just wanted to hear a friendly voice.'

'Cracked it yet?'

'You're joking. I'm getting nowhere. I seem to be driving here, there and everywhere and achieving nothing.'

'You must have eliminated some people.'

'I don't know any more. I'm chasing a very shadowy murderer, if such a person even exists.'

'OK, so you're on a downer. That's your usual pattern. Can't you put a spin on it like politicians do?'

'I'm not in the mood,' I said. 'Fran hasn't contacted me and I want to talk to her daughter at her boarding school but I doubt Neil, the father, will agree to me talking to her.'

'I'll get Peace Haven's number from my contact,' said Hubert. 'And at the school you can say you're the nit nurse.'

'People aren't that trusting these days.'

'You'll just have to blag it.'

'You're making me smile,' I said. 'Will you ring Peace Haven for me and get Fran to give me ring?'

'I'll do anything to have you home that bit quicker. Jasper's missing you.'

As I clicked the off button on my mobile phone I felt a surge of homesickness. Hubert was my anchor in a stormy sea and my harbour was Longborough, and although it could be dull I missed its calm sameness. Only Hubert seemed to stay a constant in my life. Simon hadn't phoned me, but then he was a serving officer and I guessed his involvement was at an end because if his superiors found out he was giving information to a PI he could lose his job.

I finally arrived in Cromer at two p.m. I found the address easily enough but the hilltop house was too steep for a car. Luckily I found a parking space and began the walk upwards. It was worth the effort. The view of the sea was spectacular. The house itself was chalet style, white and glimmering in the spring sunshine. There was a porch with a swinging seat and I felt sorry that Fiona couldn't enjoy more time here instead of being sent away to school.

Neil answered the door after I'd rung the bell several times. He was tall, quite rugged looking, unshaven for some days and wearing one of those fisherman's tops with deep pockets. The stubble and the paint splashes on his top gave him the appearance of an artist at work. As I explained my mission his warm smile faded.

'You look the determined type,' he said coldly. 'You'd better come in and explain.'

He led me through to the lounge, which was light, airy and modern. The picture windows looked out over the sea and a sofa and an armchair faced the view. To me it seemed the sort of house an older couple would buy and spend large parts of the day staring out to the ever-changing view. There were two vases of fresh flowers in the room, to me a sure indication that there was a woman either living with him or visiting on a bed and breakfast basis.

'Have I got my facts right?' he said. 'You're investigating the death of my son because you think my ex-wife wasn't responsible.'

'You've got it in one, Mr Rowley.'

'Do sit down,' he said. 'And tell me what evidence you could possibly have to suggest my wife — ex-wife — wasn't guilty even though she pleaded guilty at the time.' He didn't give me time to answer but asked, 'Tea, coffee?' I shook my head. 'I'll make a pot of tea,' he said. 'You can work on your argument.'

While he was out of the room I wandered around looking for a photograph of Fiona but there were no knick-knacks. On the walls were several oil paintings, mostly of cubes and triangles except for one about a foot square of a young girl on a beach staring out to sea. I thought it was quite striking. The girl looked like Fran but I guessed it was Fiona.

'That's Fiona,' Neil said as he entered the room carrying a tray of tea. 'She's at boarding school.'

'I'm surprised you sent her away after the trauma she'd suffered.'

'Really? I don't think sending an only child "away" as you say, is detrimental. In fact she begged to go.'

'Didn't she like your new girlfriend?'

He scowled. 'You're being very irritating. Tea?'

This time I nodded. I studied Neil while he poured the tea. He was good-looking and the one smile I'd seen was attractive; his voice was sexy but I found his pompous manner grating.

'You were going to tell me about new evidence,' he said as he handed me a mug of tea.

I swallowed hard. I hadn't got one shred of actual evidence. I had one or two options. The first was to pass out and feign illness, the second was to blag it as Hubert had suggested.

I decided on the second option. 'The evidence I have already,' I began confidently, 'will be passed on to the police in due course. I can't discuss it with anyone until then.'

'I understand that,' he said quietly. 'But I'm shocked that after all this time you've managed to cast doubt on Fran's guilt.'

He sat down and put a hand to his head. 'I've seen Claudette,' I said, 'and she's told me about her heroin habit and Erin's drug-running activities. You, of course, were cheating on your wife and, it seems, skiving off in the day and most evenings.'

His expression was now hangdog. 'That's all true,' he said. 'I did love Fran, you know, but she was always preoccupied — her work, then the children and I came last.'

'She had to concentrate on her work,' I snapped. 'After all she was the chief breadwinner.'

'If you must know I was a lousy accountant. I made a major cock-up and cost the firm several grand. They gave me an offer I couldn't refuse — resign or be fired.'

'You never told Fran?'

'No. I didn't want her to think badly of me so I made up a pack of lies about following my dream of being an artist. I don't kid myself; I know I only have a little talent but I had to do something to while away the hours.'

'That and the odd affair,' I said, staring at him.

He stared back at me and then looked away. For the first time his face showed signs of remorse. 'I was lonely,' he said softly. 'I wanted Fran, I loved her. But she was always too tired or stressed to make love — so I looked elsewhere.'

'That must have been a real hardship,' I said.

'I wasn't just screwing around,' he snapped back. 'I did sell some of my paintings and every day I tried to find a proper job but the world of accountancy is quite small in London and no firm would even interview me.'

'Fair enough,' I conceded. 'Let's talk about Fran now. Why did you shun her so completely? She took the blame for her son's death and stayed silent about your . . . activities. In the media you were a "new man" while Fran was a hard-hearted career woman driven to kill. It seems to me she could have pleaded guilty to manslaughter—'

'I know, I know,' he interrupted me. 'We were all in shock. I think she was advised badly by her legal team. I'd lost my son, my wife had admitted killing him and Fifi was virtually struck dumb. I wasn't thinking straight.'

'No, and neither was Fran. She took full responsibility as she had done since Fiona was born.'

'This is getting us nowhere,' he said angrily. 'That night there was no break-in. Only Fran and Fifi were in the house. It must have been Fran — there's no doubt.'

'She doesn't remember doing it.'

'Who would want to remember something like that? Get real.'

'Claudette had a key to the front door and so did Erin. Who else could have had a key?

'I don't bloody know! You're not suggesting that Fran's sister had anything to do with Ben's death, are you?'

'It's no more unlikely that Fran herself. A jealous sister in a rage—'

'No,' he snapped. 'You're talking rubbish.'

I was just about to reply to that when my mobile phone rang.

'You carry on,' he said. 'I need some fresh air.' He stomped off and, feeling relieved, I answered my call. It was Hubert.

'I've got some news,' he said. He was using his funereal voice so I knew it was serious.

CHAPTER THIRTY

'Tell me, Hubert, what's happened?' I asked.

'Fran never made it to Peace Haven,' he said loudly as if I were deaf. 'I'm getting in touch with all the taxi drivers in the area but no luck so far.'

'I presume she's gone back to the cottage,' I said. Then I muttered under my breath, 'Silly bitch.'

'What was that?'

'Nothing. Thanks for your efforts.'

'What will you do now?' he asked.

'I can't go chasing after her at the moment. I'll have to try to speak to her daughter before I leave Norfolk.'

'How's Neil Rowley reacting to all this?'

'He's getting some fresh air at the moment but I think I can persuade him to allow me to see Fiona.'

'If it's a problem I could drive to Woburn to check on Fran.'

'That might freak her out. I'll manage to be there tomorrow . . .' I tailed off.

'What's the matter?' asked Hubert anxiously.

'I just wonder why she doesn't answer her mobile. I've left messages.'

'You could try her land line.'

'I'll do that. Thanks.'

Hubert's call left me feeling uneasy. Fran was behaving strangely; I could understand her not wanting to go back to Peace Haven but why the hell wasn't she answering my calls?

Neil's return gave me no more time to think and I didn't feel I could spend much more time with him; after all it was Fiona I wanted to see. I put it to him bluntly. 'I need to see your daughter, today if possible.'

'Out of the question,' he snapped. 'She doesn't remember anything. She was only five at the time.'

'Has anyone asked her about that night since the court case, I mean?'

'We don't talk about it, we never have.'

'She's bound to ask questions now that she's older.'

'It's no good arguing with me. I don't want her upset.'

He looked away and I caught an expression of embarrassment. 'You're not telling me the truth, are you?' I said.

'You think you could have handled this better, do you? What the hell do you say to a five-year-old who has seen her baby brother murdered by her mother?'

'What did you say?'

He sighed deeply. 'If you must know, Fiona was told her mother and brother died of an illness. How can I *now* tell her mother is still alive?'

'She'll find out eventually and then she'll feel you betrayed her.'

'I'll deal with it when the time comes.'

I thought quickly. If I lost this chance now I might not get another. 'I could talk to your daughter on a pretext.'

'What do you mean?'

'I could say I was a writer interested in traumatic childhood memories. I don't have to mention Fran. I'll let Fiona talk.'

'No. I've made up my mind. We never mention it. Maybe she's forgotten about that night.'

'What about her nightmares?'

'You know about those, do you? Yes, she does wake in the night. Sometimes she screams out and talks nonsense about white flowers.'

'What if it isn't nonsense?'

'Of course it is. She's thinking about funerals, that's all.'

'That's a possibility,' I agreed. 'But until someone asks her, the nightmares will continue.'

'You are wasting your time,' he said. 'My answer is still emphatically no.'

Even I know when I hit a brick wall head on so I thanked him and left my business card in case he changed his mind. I walked back to my car wondering how I could penetrate a boarding school's walls. How many days would I have to hang around waiting for a glimpse of Fiona? Then it dawned on me that all I had to do was to get a note to her. How I would word this note and where I would meet her remained unknown but the written word might prevail.

My optimism faded when I saw the school. Surrounded by lawns and with a long exposed driveway my car would instantly be seen. There was a large clock tower to the right of the quadrangle and the main school building was a mixture of Victorian elegance combined with ugly modern extensions. I drove past the entrance and managed to park a few hundred yards away where I began to write the few lines that I hoped would interest Fiona enough to meet me.

On a sheet of my notepaper I wrote:

Dear Fiona,
My name is Kate and I was a friend of your mother's. I have just returned from abroad. I have spoken to your father and he doesn't approve of my seeing you but Fran was a dear friend and I would love to take you out to tea. Can you plan an escape? If so I could meet you at the school gates at a time to suit you. If you're interested please ring me on Tel . . .

I had to copy my mobile phone number from my diary but once signed I folded it carefully and then rummaged in my suitcase for an envelope. I didn't have one but I did have a small roll of sellotape. The finished effort wasn't impressive but I hoped Fiona would at least be intrigued. Finding a messenger might prove difficult but I was determined to seek out a likely-looking candidate.

A clipboard looks businesslike if caught out skulking around any building and so, armed with a clipboard and pen I walked down the gravel path towards the school. There was no one about so I walked confidently as if I had every right to be there. It was just after four and there was still no sign of any schoolgirls. Eventually I settled behind a clump of bushes near the car park. I waited and waited and then at five o'clock there was a noisy release of students into the quadrangle.

I skirted the quad looking in vain for Fiona amongst the uniformed girls who seemed different only in height. I stood watching as most began to disperse to the various new one-storey buildings. They seemed oblivious to my presence but there's always one who is different, and she was. Taller than the others with long fair hair in a pony tail she seemed to be marshalling the younger ones. I hoped she was a sixth former and not a member of staff. I caught her eye and she came over to me.

'Can I help you?' she asked politely.

'I'm looking for Fiona Rowley. I have a message for her. I wanted to find someone to deliver it to her.' I handed her the unimpressive-looking note. She took it but I noticed in her eyes a vague suspicion.

'Wait here,' she said.

I actually waited by the clock tower, leaning on it and trying to look both nonchalant and businesslike with my clipboard in one hand and my pen in the other. The giggling and high-pitched voices were quiet now. There wasn't a soul in the quadrangle.

A few minutes later I heard voices. I peered round a corner of the clock tower to see Miss Tall the sixth former, an older man and a large woman looking suspiciously like the headmistress or matron advancing on me. I looked towards the school entrance and decided I had no choice but to leg it. I began running as fast as I could but the sixth former had legs and a body made for running. Already my legs felt wooden but I wasn't prepared to let them catch me. Miss Tall was right behind me. I speeded up and so did she. Then she made her move.

CHAPTER THIRTY-ONE

She tried to grab me. Unfortunately for her she missed her footing and fell heavily. I carried on running and didn't look back until I reached the safety of my car. Even then I accelerated away at speed. I drove for about half a mile and only then did I stop to catch my breath.

Another fine mess, I thought, but it was getting late and I needed to book into a hotel or decide if I had the strength to drive to Fran's cottage. I chose not to drive. I was in no fit state and I hoped maybe she'd answer her land line.

On the outskirts of Cromer I saw a B&B with a vacancies sign up. The Coral Guest House. It looked OK with whitewashed walls and potted plants at either side of the front door and a couple of ornamental butterflies decorating the walls. The owner, Coral Hill, was verging on sixty, had heavy swollen legs but a medium-sized top half. Her face was red and little rivulets of perspiration coursed down from her forehead. 'I've only got one room to let.' she said. 'It's usually empty because it's next door to my mother's room and it can be a little noisy so if you'd rather look elsewhere I'll understand.' I decided to take a chance on the grounds that I couldn't be bothered doing anything else.

The room itself was on the ground floor and was a symphony of pink chintz. There was an en-suite shower room where even the spare toilet roll was encased in a pink crocheted dress. I sat on the bed and punched out Fran's number at the cottage. I let it ring and ring. There was no reply. The only other place I could think of where Fran would stay was with her one friend and ally. I rummaged in my bag for his business card and was about to ring him when my mobile phone rang with its lively new cock-a-doodle-do ring tone. It was Hubert. He wasted no time.

'Fran isn't at the cottage. I rang the estate manager and he's just let me know that all her belongings have gone.'

'Thanks,' I said. 'I think she's staying with Malcolm.'

'Have you got his number?'

'Actually I have. I'll ring him.'

We chatted for a few more minutes, mostly about Jasper. Then Hubert said, 'Simon phoned me; he'd lost your number. His mother's now in a nursing home. She's quite poorly. I gave him your new mobile number so expect a call.'

'At least it wasn't personal.'

'You'd make a fine wife for any man,' said Hubert, 'and don't you forget that.'

'I don't think Simon is the one,' I said.

'You're too fussy. Take care.'

The Coral Guest House didn't provide an evening meal so I decided to try some local fish and chips. I chose The Plaice because the queue was long and although I had to wait twenty minutes I was sure it was worth the wait. I sat in my car, ate my delicious fish and chips, swallowed my guilt and drove straight back to the Coral.

In my room I rang Malcolm. He replied almost immediately.

'Is Fran with you?' I asked bluntly.

'No. Has something happened? She's supposed to have gone back to Peace Haven.'

'She's missing.'

'Where would she go?' he asked.

'I thought you might be able to tell me. I'm quite worried now.'

'I'm sorry, Kate, I'm as puzzled and worried as you are. I've no idea.'

He sounded genuine so that was my one and only instinct about Fran's disappearance squashed like a fly. Was this the end of it? Fran could have used her mobile to ring me but she hadn't bothered. Neither Neil nor Fiona was interested. Even Malcolm seemed half-hearted. I guessed having a sick wife and an important job was as much as he could cope with. And yet he had been Fran's only visitor in prison.

It was then that the noise started up from next door. 'Mother! Stop it, it's time for bed.' I recognized Coral's voice.

'Leave me alone, you bitch,' a querulous voice retorted.

'It's Coral. I'm your daughter.'

'You're lying. I don't know you.'

'Come on, Mum. Let's get your clothes off.'

'Police! Police, call the police!'

'You like your bed,' said Coral in a loud voice.

'My own bed, not this one. I want my own bed.'

'You're been in this bed for four years. It is your own bed.'

'Leave me alone.'

'Bill,' Coral shouted. 'Come and give me a hand.'

Heavy footsteps heralded Bill's approach. His voice was a few decibels louder than Coral's. 'Come on then, madam. You know me. It's Bill. And it's time you were in bed.'

The old lady began to cry then but twenty minutes or so later I heard the door shut and all was silent.

I had just snuggled down to sleep when my mobile rang. I knew it wasn't Hubert; he'd never ring so late.

'Hello?'

'Is that Kate?' The voice was young and small, barely above a whisper.

'Yes. Is that Fiona?'

'My mother's not dead, is she?'

I took a deep breath before replying. 'No, she isn't. Your father—'

'I hate her. I hate them both. I don't want to see either of them ever again.'

'I only wanted to talk to you,' I said softly. 'You don't have to see your mother.'

There was such a long pause that I began to wonder if she was still on the line.

'Where is my mother?' she asked.

'I don't know,' I said. 'She's . . . gone away for a few days.'

'Good.'

With that the line went dead. I felt that I hadn't handled Fiona's call too well and although her words suggested she wasn't interested she had been motivated enough to call me. I got ready for bed and told myself that if I could prove Fran's innocence then Fiona would be fine.

Sleep was about to overtake me when I heard a door opening. A second later my door handle was rattled. I was rattled too but I guessed it was Coral's mum. She was most persistent and began kicking at my door. I jumped out of bed and opened the door. She was quite scary, toothless with straggles of fine white hair and a pallor that matched her white nightie. 'There's my bed,' she said and before I could stop her she'd climbed into it.

I managed to find the owners in their extended kitchen which appeared to function as one big multi-purpose room. They were sitting on a sofa in their nightclothes watching television and were hugely apologetic as they bustled me back to my room.

'I'm so sorry about this,' Coral kept saying. In my bed Coral's mother slept soundly and it took both Coral and Bill a few minutes to sit her up and then haul her to her feet and frogmarch her from the room.

From then on real sleep evaded me and I was up, showered, dressed and ready to go by six thirty a.m. I left cash for my night's stay by the hall phone and minus my full English breakfast I began the drive back to London.

* * *

London seemed muggy and humid after the fresh sea air of Cromer but I didn't plan to stay long. I'd decided that haring around England was becoming tiring and unproductive — I wanted to go home.

My first stop was back to Hunter, Hunter and Blaze. Somehow I felt the answer must lie with that place and the people Fran spent most of her time with. Today there was a different receptionist. Andrea was in her mid-thirties and had a genuine smile and a pretty face. I introduced myself and asked if she'd been working there when Fran was employed.

'I was a secretary then,' she said. 'I left to have a baby. I've been back about three years now. I'm only part-time and this job was forced on me, but I like it so . . .' She gave a little shrug.

'When Fran worked here,' I said, 'did she ever seem troubled by stalkers or threatening letters?'

Andrea thought for a moment. 'I don't know anything about threatening letters but she did have an admirer. Everyone knew about it except for Fran. She didn't seem to notice, or if she did she didn't care.'

'Notice what?'

'Malcolm Talgarth was nuts about her. I'm sorry to say we all sniggered about it. If she left the building he was seconds behind her. They had an office adjacent to each other so I suppose he heard her door click shut as she left her office.'

'He's a married man, isn't he?'

'Yes, but his wife's been ill for years . . .' She paused. 'Office gossip was that they were having an affair, but she wasn't the type.

'Is Malcolm in today?'

'He came through earlier,' she said, 'and I haven't seen him leave. I believe he's doing some work from home.'

A sudden influx of people to the reception desk gave me an excuse to thank her and leave abruptly. Outside I paused on the pavement. I'd judged Fran as being cool under fire and in control. Now I was beginning to see that she was weak in one area. All the evidence pointed to it but I'd been so busy thinking of her as victim of an indifferent husband that I hadn't seen her obvious flaw.

I hailed a taxi and within twenty minutes I was outside Malcolm's gloomy house. I rapped the door knocker several times but there was no reply. I yelled Fran's name through the letter box several times but again there was no reply. Finally I tried yelling for Malcolm too. Silence.

I was getting into the house one way or the other. I searched for a hidden spare key under bricks and flower pots but there wasn't one. At the back of the house the top half of the kitchen door was glass. I took off my shoe and tried to smash it. That didn't work. I looked around for something stronger with which to smash the glass. There was a shed at the top of the garden and in there I found a spade. The spade worked but the sound of breaking glass seemed loud enough to alert half the neighbourhood. I waited a few seconds expecting some response but there was none inside or outside.

Once inside the kitchen I began calling out. I searched the ground floor calling Fran's name and soon it began to sound more like a lament. The stairs were wide and poorly lit and as I ascended them a shiver crept up my back.

CHAPTER THIRTY-TWO

At the top of the stairs I stopped and struggled to find a light switch. There was no natural light but there was an unnatural silence and yet I was convinced someone was in the house. With the light switched on I breathed a sigh of relief. I stopped calling Fran's name and began opening doors. The first of the four doors leading from the landing was the bathroom, then a totally empty room and then the darkened room where in the middle of a double bed a woman lay fast asleep.

I stood over the bed and for a few seconds stared at the deeply asleep Fran.

'Fran,' I called, shaking her by the shoulder. 'Wake up. We've got to get out of here.' I pinched her ear lobes, a nurse's trick to rouse the semi-conscious, but that too failed. I ran to the bathroom and filled a tooth mug with cold water and then threw that over her face. This time she did rouse enough to say, 'Piss off — leave me alone.'

'It's Kate. Come on, wake up! What's happened? What have you taken?'

She shook her head as if trying to think. I hauled her into the upright position but she fell to one side. There was only one decision I could make. Fran needed an ambulance.

I sat down so that Fran was propped against me and began punching out 999. I didn't manage the final 9 because Fran grabbed my wrist and said falteringly, 'No, no hospital . . . I don't want to be . . . certified.'

'What have you taken?' I asked.

With a real effort of will Fran moved herself into the upright position. 'I'm scared,' she slurred. 'I'm seeing things . . . hearing things . . . I can't think straight.'

'We have to get out of here,' I said, trying to sound calm. 'Malcolm might come back at any time.'

'He says . . .' She broke off as if struggling for the right words. 'He says I've had a breakdown.'

'Can you stand?' I asked in reply, knowing this was no time to discuss her mental health.

'I think so.'

She was wearing a white Victorian nightie that reached to her ankles. It would have to do; I wasn't prepared to waste any time. With my support she managed to get to the door. We were about to make slow progress towards the stairs when she said, 'What about Maria?'

'Maria?' I queried.

'Malcolm's wife.'

'Where is she?'

'She's dangerous. She wants to kill me and Malcolm.'

'Where is she?' I repeated.

'The next room to me. He keeps it locked.'

'You've heard her?'

'I think so.' Her head nodded forward as if the effort of keeping it upright was impossible. Her body was as floppy as a rag doll and her brain was in the same state. I sat her down with her back against the wall but I didn't rush towards that room. I was sure that behind the locked door lay a body and I would have preferred to have made a dash for it. So I walked slowly.

The door was locked but not by a key. There were two bolts at the top and bottom of the door. They were new and shiny. I had to stretch to reach the top one and at first it wouldn't slide. It took three attempts but eventually the door was unbolted. I glanced along the landing to where Fran was slumped and leaning to one side. I took my mobile from my pocket and dialled 999. The operator told me an ambulance would be there 'as soon as possible' and I was to try to keep the patient talking until the paramedics arrived. I glanced at my watch. It was nearly one o'clock. Lunch time. Heavy traffic.

I took a deep breath as I put my hand on the door handle. Heavy curtains kept out the light. The room was cold and the smell was foetid, a mixture of stale urine and body odour. I felt for the light switch and clicked it on. A bare low-wattage bulb gave off a shadowy light. Lying on a single bed was a huddled heap. I approached cautiously. I was scared and my heart rate was already far too fast. As I got nearer I caught a glimpse of hair from beneath the duvet. I tried to stifle my fear by telling myself that I'd seen dead bodies before, but it didn't help.

I lifted the duvet from Maria's face. She lay on her side, her sunken eyes closed. I touched the skin of her arm. My finger left an indentation. She was cold. Her lips were cracked and bloody. In that instant her eyes sprang open. Her lips moved. She was trying to speak. I knelt down so that I could hear her. 'Water,' she was saying. 'Water . . . water.'

This time I did rush. I ran to the bathroom, filled a tooth mug with water and rushed back. Fran still sat immobile. I moved Maria slightly so that she could drink some of the water but she was so thirsty I had to stop her gulping too fast and having too much at once.

'You're safe now,' I said. She closed her eyes and clung on to my hand. It was now one ten p.m. It seemed a lifetime since I'd last checked looked at my watch.

When I heard the front door open I felt sick. I let go of Maria's hand and felt in my pocket for my mobile phone. It wasn't there. Malcolm's footsteps already sounded on the stairs.

'Fran,' I heard him say, 'why are you out of bed? You know you're not well.'

From somewhere my anger became courage. I had to protect two women from this evil bastard.

I stood arms akimbo outside Maria's room. 'The police and an ambulance are on their way. I'm warning you now I'm trained in martial arts. I'll break every bone in your body.'

He stepped over Fran's legs and advanced towards me. He stood in front of me looking menacing and my bravado slipped away like a sliver of ice down a hot throat.

'You stupid bitch,' he said calmly. 'I had everything planned and now I've got to change those plans.' I was watching him intently and working out my next move when he punched me in the stomach. The blow, so sudden and unexpected, had me bent double, unable to breathe. I became light-headed and that was followed by wave after wave of nausea. A punch to my face felled me. If I was unconscious it didn't last long because I was aware of banging sounds coming from downstairs. Then he hit me again.

I came to in a dark room. I was disorientated, my jaw was stiff, one eye was half closed. I was lying down next to Fran, who appeared to be asleep. I managed to get myself upright by getting on to my knees. I gasped in shock when a thin white hand seemed to appear from nowhere. It took me a moment to realize it was Maria's hand and she was trying to help me up.

Once on my feet I felt dizzy but I staggered to the bedroom door as if I believed that was our way out. He had, of course, bolted us in. I stared at my watch like a small child still learning to tell the time. When my eyes and my brain were eventually working in tandem I could see that it was two ten. I remembered that I'd called for an ambulance. Had they been? Had Malcolm fobbed them off? I walked over to the window and pulled back the curtains. The sudden light made me squint and as my eyes focused disappointment followed. The window faced the garden. There would be no passers-by to see our plight.

CHAPTER THIRTY-THREE

Fran began to make little moaning noises so I left the window and pulled her into the upright position.

'For God's sake wake up, Fran,' I said. 'We've got to get out of here.'

She opened her eyes. 'What's happened? What's going on?' Her voice was less slurred now but she was obviously still groggy.

'Your fine friend Malcolm has us locked in. Maria's very ill, she's dehydrated and starving. We have to get out of here quickly to save her life . . .'

Fran looked around trying to focus her eyes. I was on my own. Whatever drugs he'd given her might take hours to wear off. 'Try to stay awake,' I said. 'Otherwise you'll die.'

I didn't think she would die but fear is a good motivator and she shook her head as if trying to get her thoughts straight. 'Where is he?' she asked.

'I don't know but I think he's still in the house.'

'Malcolm drinks a lot,' she muttered.

'Let's hope he drinks a bucketful.'

I went back to the window. It was a sash window. I knew it wouldn't open because some dickhead had painted it badly. I still tried but it was no use. I needed to smash the window but what with? I was wearing trainers; Fran and Maria had no footwear. I looked around the room. The only items available as any sort of window-smashing device were a small wardrobe and a bedside table. If Fran roused herself, between the two of us I was convinced we could ram the cupboard at the window. It would be noisy but it might work. The sound of breaking glass might also be enough to alert Malcolm. What the hell was he doing anyway? And who would come to our aid? The garden was surrounded by evergreens and although I could see the window of a house the occupants were probably out working.

Maria remained semi-conscious. I took her pulse; it was rapid and irregular, her breathing shallow. If I needed motivation then she was it. I still hesitated but not for long. The sound of the bolts drawing back caused me to hold my breath, hoping it was rescue but fearing Malcolm instead. It was Malcolm. He carried a bundle of clothes and a pair of shoes which he threw on the floor.

'Get dressed, Fran.' He pointed at me. 'You help her. You've got five minutes.'

Fran looked scared but she had the courage to say 'no', loudly.

'Don't argue,' he said. 'We're going abroad, sweetheart. You'll soon be well.'

'I'm not ill,' she said defiantly.

'Get dressed,' he said calmly. 'Or I'll kill Maria. She'll die quickly with a pillow over her face; she'll be dead in seconds.'

'Just like Benjamin,' I said quietly.

'Exactly,' he said, unperturbed.

I caught the expression on Fran's face. It was a mixture of shock and rage. 'Why?' she asked. 'Why?'

Malcolm shrugged. 'He was crying; he wouldn't stop. I didn't want him to wake you. You were sound asleep.'

Poor Fran struggled for words that wouldn't come.

'You bastard!' I snapped. 'Fran went to prison for your crime.'

'I did advise her to plead not guilty,' he said. 'My plan went wrong. I'd planned a plea of not guilty whilst the balance of the mind was disturbed. That way she'd have been treated in a psychiatric hospital for a year and then she'd have been out and free. But she wasn't guided by me. And after all, in our new life together I didn't want the boy tagging along and looking more like his father every day.'

'And Maria?' I asked, my mouth dry with fear.

'The bitch wouldn't die. I wanted her to die of natural causes like my first wife. She was mentally ill too. A very difficult woman, but in the end I won. In contrast Maria has been strangely resilient.'

I was lost for words. Fran had begun to get herself dressed. I helped her take off her nightie and put on a bra and jumper. Her eyes were bright now, bright with anger, but her body was still slow.

'Come on,' he urged. 'Come on.' He still stood in the doorway and I did wonder if I should try to tackle him but remembering my failure before I hesitated.

It was then that the cock crowed. Or to be accurate my cock-a-doodle-doo ring tone sounded. 'What the hell is that?' he asked.

'It's my mobile. If I don't answer it my partner calls the police.'

'Where is it?'

'Next door.'

He strode across and grabbed my arm, forcing it behind my back. 'Answer it and say nothing except you're busy and you'll ring back.'

He marched me into the next room where I'd left my phone by Fran's bed.

'There you are,' said Hubert when I managed to say 'Hello'.

'Where are you?'

'I'm busy, Harry,' I said. 'I'll ring you . . .'

I prayed Hubert would now know I was in trouble.

Malcolm snatched the phone from me, pressed the red off button and threw the phone across the floor.

Fran had managed to finish dressing and had been able to prop herself against a wall. He let go of me and took Fran's arm. She flopped against him. 'Stand up properly, my darling,' he said, trying to drag her out. I saw my chance and I ran towards the door but he was after me in a second. He grabbed my legs and we both landed on the floor. I tried to fight. I scratched his face, pulled his hair but then he sat on my chest and I really thought I would die. Instead of fighting I was scrabbling, trying to get my breath, trying to survive.

Everything went black, then suddenly the weight was gone from my chest and I could breathe again in fierce gasps.

When I'd stopped seeing stars I saw that Malcolm was trying to drag a resisting Fran across the room. She'd lost a shoe but she managed to grab it as she was being dragged along by one arm. With the shoe she was whacking him on the legs. I got on to my knees slowly, feeling dizzy and light-headed. Malcolm hauled Fran to her feet and slapped her hard across the face. I tried to stand up but all I could do was crawl across the room to the shoe just as he closed the door. I half stood and managed to grab the door handle. On the other side of the door Malcolm seemed to be losing his icy calm.

'You stupid bitch,' he shouted. 'Get up! I'm trying to help you. I'm going to look after you.' For a few seconds there was silence then it sounded as if they were moving away from the door.

I opened the door a fraction and saw they were at the top of the stairs. He had hold of Fran's arm but she started to sag and then collapsed in a heap. I was fairly certain she was merely playing for time. He was standing by the stairs telling her to cooperate. I swung the door open and ran at him. He turned to look at me running towards him but taken by surprise he didn't realize he was so close to the stairs. Fran stuck her leg out and he tripped, lost his footing and went hurtling downwards. I only just managed to stop in time.

Fran stood up and we both peered down the stairs. One of his legs lay at an awkward angle. There was a strong possibility he was still alive. I didn't plan to investigate his condition but Fran did. In her desperation to get to him she sat on her bottom and bumped her way down the stairs. I was torn between phoning for the police and following her. As I turned to run for my mobile phone I heard Fran screaming, 'You bastard. I'm going to kill you.'

I tore down the stairs as she hammered him with her shoe. She'd hit him several times before I grabbed the shoe from her. 'Don't kill him,' I shouted. 'He's your evidence.'

She collapsed in tears as someone banged at the door. It was two paramedics closely followed by the police.

One of the paramedics bent over the prone figure lying on the floor. 'Is he dead?' cried Fran plaintively.

CHAPTER THIRTY-FOUR

'No, love,' said the paramedic, kneeling at our enemy to feel his pulse and put an oxygen mask on his face. 'His pulse is strong and he's breathing OK.'

'Upstairs,' I said, 'is a very sick woman. She's dehydrated and she's been starved.'

'We'll sort it, sweetheart,' said the older paramedic calmly.

Then the police appeared in assorted ranks and sizes. Maria and Fran were taken to hospital accompanied by a policewoman. I refused to go. I felt in need of a stiff brandy and I wouldn't get that in hospital.

One of the cops — a tall guy with a friendly face — put an arm round me and led me to a police car. Within minutes I was sitting in an interview room with a hot sweet cup of tea and it seemed even more surreal than being with mad Malcolm.

'Now then,' said a Detective Inspector Nelson Potter. His partner was a DS Ruth Stone who smiled a lot and seemed to be chief tea supplier.

'Tell me about it from the beginning,' he said.

An hour later I was still talking and his eyes were beginning to glaze over. I even told him about David being killed. I was aware I was talking too much but I couldn't stop myself.

DS Stone was following my garbled but long-winded account quite well, I thought.

'So, in a nutshell,' she said with a smile, 'you're telling us that Malcolm Talgarth murdered Benjamin Rowley and let Mrs Rowley take the blame, then when she got out of prison he drugged her, half-starved and drugged his wife, and in all probability murdered his first wife.'

'Yes. Precisely.'

'Wow,' she said.

DI Potter looked a little worried. 'We'll need a full and comprehensive written report from you as soon as possible.'

'Not today,' I said. 'I want to see Fran and Maria.'

'We'll take you to them,' he said.

'Now?'

'Certainly.' I guessed he was glad to get me out of the building.

DS Stone drove me to the hospital. On the way she lent me her mobile phone; mine was probably bagged up and was either in lost property or some forensic department. I rang Hubert. His phone went straight to voicemail. I tried him again as we parked just outside the A&E department.

'I've been worried sick,' he said. 'Are you OK? Did the police get there in time?'

'You rang them?'

'Well, it wasn't the tooth fairy. Of course I rang them. I'm on my way. Take care.'

Bit late for that, I thought, but I was grateful that he was coming. I'd talked myself dry and now I felt shivery and nauseous.

In the A&E department DS Stone sat me down in a waiting bay and said she'd get us some coffee. Minutes later a Dr Daniel Cole appeared with Ruth Stone by his side.

'We need to check you over,' he said.

'I'm only visiting,' I protested.

Dr Cole wasn't deterred. 'It will only take a few minutes and you can see your friends while you wait.'

'Wait for what?' I asked.

'Your jaw needs an X-ray and your eye needs looking at.'

'There's nothing wrong with me.'

It was then that DS Stone handed me a compact mirror. My face was a mess. One eye was half closed, my upper lip was swollen to twice its size and there were various bruises over my cheeks. It wasn't the first time my face had been mashed and I did know that in a few days I'd look nearly normal. My facial state, combined with the various aches and pains I was now feeling, forced me to stop protesting.

I was directed to a curtained bay and told to lie down on a trolley. Ruth Stone sat on a chair beside me and within minutes a nurse came to check if my vital signs were still vital (they were) and while I waited for my X-ray I was allowed to see Fran, who was in the next bay.

The fact that there was a policewoman by my side deterred me from saying too much. Fran looked pale and distraught. I whispered in her ear, 'Have you told them you're pregnant?'

She nodded and a single tear slipped down her cheek. 'They're not sure if the baby is still alive.'

We didn't say much. Fran kept apologising for not telling me the whole truth and I told her not to worry. It was all very superficial but neither of us was fit enough for anything more.

Maria too was still in the department. She lay on a trolley with an intravenous drip in place and a young nurse by her side. She'd been washed and wore a clean hospital nightie. Her raw lips had been coated with salve and she seemed to be in a peaceful sleep. I was about to leave when her eyes opened. 'Thank you,' she said. 'Is he dead?'

'No. The police are with him. He can't hurt you now.'

'I'm not mad, am I?'

'No,' I said. 'You're not mad. He's the mad one.'

She smiled weakly and then closed her eyes.

The tragedy of the two women's shattered lives suddenly hit me and I started to cry. I didn't stop for several minutes. By the time Hubert arrived I looked worse than I had before.

He didn't question me on the way back to Longborough. He didn't get much chance because I slept all the way home. Once home I made a big fuss of Jasper and went straight to bed. Hubert had his disappointed face on but I was exhausted. As I lay in bed I remembered my car was still in Southgate and my investigation had numerous strands that still needed to be sorted. Sheer tiredness overcame my niggling worries and I just slept and slept.

It was ten in the morning before I emerged. In the kitchen Hubert sat looking like a condemned man. When he saw me he did manage a smile. 'I've worried about you,' he said. 'I thought you might have slipped into a coma.'

'No such luck.' I said. 'What's for breakfast? I'm starving.'

'There is a God,' said Hubert. 'You're back to normal.'

Hubert's breakfast cholesterol may have been harmful in the long term but in the short term it was well worth the risk.

'Now you've been fed,' he said, 'you can tell me what happened.'

I censored the bit about me being a martial arts expert because I didn't want to seem completely stupid and when I'd finished he said, 'Your trouble is, Kate, you do seem to think your clients can do no wrong.'

'I have to think the best *of* them otherwise I couldn't do my best *for* them.'

'That's as may be but try to not to let your emotions get in the way.'

'Yeah, yeah,' I said. 'Anyway it's not over yet. I need to speak to Fran and find out what the hell she was playing at with that creep.'

'And then what?'

'I want to keep in touch with Maria. She seems to be all alone in the world—'

'Enough,' he interrupted me. 'You can't solve everyone's problems.'

'I'll have a damn good try,' I said.

A little later I rang Fran's sister Claudette to tell her what had happened. She said very little and I suggested she rang the hospital to find out when she was being discharged. She was non-committal and I couldn't help feeling disappointed.

* * *

Hubert called it delayed shock but for the next three days I just wanted to sleep. I did manage to phone the hospital. Maria's condition was described as 'poorly but stable', Fran was discharged after twenty-four hours, and her sister had collected her.

Once my sleep fest was over I wanted to be on the move but Hubert insisted he would drive me wherever I wanted to go. My face was much less swollen and with make-up on I looked reasonable. It was about eleven a.m. when my door-bell rang. I made my way slowly downstairs where a delivery man presented me with a huge bouquet of flowers. There was a message: *Staying in Harpenden. Love Fran.*

An hour later Fran rang me. She thanked me profusely and then invited me to visit at the weekend.

'You sound really excited,' I said.

'I am. I've spoken to Neil. He's going to bring Fiona to see me on Saturday.'

'That's wonderful. How are you and Claudette getting on?'

'We've got lots to talk about but it'll be fine.'

I felt happy for Fran but for me there was still a sense of anti-climax.

When Hubert came back from a funeral he sensed my mood. 'Your trouble is you can't let go,' he said as he opened a bottle of sherry. 'Your cases are your babies and once they've flown the nest you feel bereft.'

'You're a poet,' I said.

'Cheer up or I'll send you back to Peace Haven,' he said, handing me a glass of pre-lunch sherry.

Thinking of the few people I'd met at Peace Haven made me realize how some people lived in fear and their only escape was to acquire a new identity and forsake their family and friends. In a way it was a form of banishment. How many, I wondered, cracked under the strain of living a lie?

'Kate?'

'What?'

'You did well.'

'It doesn't feel like that,' I said.

* * *

On Saturday afternoon Hubert drove me to Harpenden. He dropped me outside the bakery and drove off to find the nearest pub for his lunch. I had instructions to take as long as I needed.

It was Claudette who answered the door. She seemed happy. 'Fiona's upstairs with Fran. Fifi's in a pre-adolescent strop but I think it will be OK. Do you mind if we leave them alone for a short time? We could go for a walk.'

We walked around Harpenden for about half an hour. The sun shone and Claudette was full of remorse for believing her sister capable of murder. I muttered that I thought that given the right set of circumstances maybe we were all capable. 'Why did you take on my sister's case then?' she asked.

'I thought the press gave her a raw deal and that far from being top dog she seemed to me to be the underdog. Mind you, sometimes I doubted. And your sister didn't tell me the whole truth.'

'She can be a little secretive,' agreed Claudette.

A little later we arrived back at the flat above the bakery. The stairs acted as a filter for delicious smells. Fran and Fiona sat together on the sofa. Fiona had long straight dark hair and wore jeans and a skimpy top. She looked at least thirteen. The atmosphere was taut. Fran stood up and gave me a hug. Fiona managed a wry smile.

'Fifi, do you fancy taking your pick from the goodies downstairs?'

'Yeah. OK,' she said. Just as she got to the door Fiona turned to look back at her mother. In that instant I saw the five-year-old she once was as Fran smiled and Fiona returned her smile.

Once they'd gone Fran sighed. Her eyes were bright. 'It's going to be all right,' she said.

'No ill effects from the drugs he gave you?' I asked. She sat down on the sofa and I joined her. She put her hand on mine. 'None,' she said. 'Except that I feel so stupid. I knew he had a key. I dropped my keys in the office once. The front door key separated from the others. It was Malcolm who picked it up. "It's mine now," he said. "And one day you'll be mine too." I was flattered by his devotion and to be honest Neil and I rarely made love by then. My fault, I guess, but Malcolm let himself in with that key one evening and we had sex on the sofa. We were both married but we were both needy. I didn't see the signs. He seemed so normal and caring and he said he'd always be there for me . . .' She broke off. Her eyes filled with tears. 'You see in a way I was responsible for Ben's death. Nothing can alter that fact.'

'You've paid the price,' I said.

'No price is high enough,' she said sadly. 'His death is something I have to live with.' Then she added, 'At least Maria is going to be all right.'

'How's Neil?' I asked.

'Confused. We managed to be polite to one another.'

'What about Fiona's nightmare about the lilies?'

Fran's hand tensed on mine. 'That night she'd come looking for me in the bedroom. Often she'd creep in beside me because Neil would come in late and sleep in the spare room. A bunch of lilies had been placed by Malcolm on the bed. They were his favourite flowers. I assume he bought them for me. Fiona never actually saw Malcolm. His visits were rare. It seems that she only remembered the flowers in her subconscious. The flowers appeared and then were gone rather like her brother. As she grew older she thought it was an omen of death.'

There was a short silence before she said, 'He must have been insane, surely?'

I shrugged. 'I think a jury would think him sane. Try not to think about him, he's done you enough harm.'

I'd wanted to ask about her pregnancy but that really wasn't my business and when we heard Claudette and Fiona talking as they walked up the stairs, I made a quick decision. I wasn't going to stay. I didn't want to stay. The three of them had enough to talk about without my being there. I felt like an interloper. I made an excuse, wished them all luck and left.

The nearest pub was a few hundred yards away. Hubert was still waiting for his meal. 'That didn't take long,' he said. 'What's the matter?'

'I feel sad and a bit empty. I don't know why.'

'I do,' said Hubert. 'It's well past your lunchtime. A good meal and the tipple of your choice will make all the difference.'

He was right, of course. Halfway through my lunch I did feel much better.

'Simon rang,' he said. 'He wondered if you'd be free tomorrow night.'

'You told him I would be, didn't you?'

Hubert smiled. 'I did not. I told him it depended on your social diary.'

'Very funny.'

'I've had more than one enquiry about your availability.'

'From men?'

'You should be so lucky.'

'Who then?'

'Would-be clients.'

I sighed. 'Give me a few days.'

As we left the pub I felt a surge of emotion I hadn't felt for ages. I slipped an arm through Hubert's and realized with a shock that that emotion was happiness.

THE END

THE JOFFE BOOKS STORY

We began in 2014 when Jasper agreed to publish his mum's much-rejected romance novel and it became a bestseller.

Since then we've grown into the largest independent publisher in the UK. We're extremely proud to publish some of the very best writers in the world, including Joy Ellis, Faith Martin, Caro Ramsay, Helen Forrester, Simon Brett and Robert Goddard. Everyone at Joffe Books loves reading and we never forget that it all begins with the magic of an author telling a story.

We are proud to publish talented first-time authors, as well as established writers whose books we love introducing to a new generation of readers.

We won Trade Publisher of the Year at the Independent Publishing Awards in 2023. We have been shortlisted for Independent Publisher of the Year at the British Book Awards for the last four years, and were shortlisted for the Diversity and Inclusivity Award at the 2022 Independent Publishing Awards. In 2023 we were shortlisted for Publisher of the Year at the RNA Industry Awards.

We built this company with your help, and we love to hear from you, so please email us about absolutely anything bookish at feedback@joffebooks.com

If you want to receive free books every Friday and hear about all our new releases, join our mailing list: www.joffebooks.com/contact

And when you tell your friends about us, just remember: it's pronounced Joffe as in coffee or toffee!

ALSO BY CHRISTINE GREEN

KATE KINSELLA MYSTERIES
Book 1: DEADLY ERRAND
Book 2: DEADLY ADMIRER
Book 3: DEADLY PRACTICE
Book 4: DEADLY PARTNERS
Book 5: DEADLY BOND
Book 6: DEADLY ECHO
Book 7: DEADLY CHOICE
Book 8: DEADLY NIGHT
Book 9: DEADLY WEB
Book 10: DEADLY RETREAT

Printed in Great Britain
by Amazon

40573943R00128